Forever Italy

Forever Italy

K.C. Hawkins

Copyright © 2009 by K.C. Hawkins.

Library of Congress Control Number: 2009906972
ISBN: Hardcover   978-1-4415-5454-3
               Softcover   978-1-4415-5453-6

All rights reserved. No part of this book may be reproduced or transmitted in any form or by any means, electronic or mechanical, including photocopying, recording, or by any information storage and retrieval system, without permission in writing from the copyright owner.

This is a work of fiction. Names, characters, places and incidents either are the product of the author's imagination or are used fictitiously, and any resemblance to any actual persons, living or dead, events, or locales is entirely coincidental.

This book was printed in the United States of America.

To order additional copies of this book, contact:
Xlibris Corporation
1-888-795-4274
www.Xlibris.com
Orders@Xlibris.com

Dedication

I dedicate this first book to myself for achieving my dream of writing and publishing this work.

I would also like to thank my peer editors for their honesty and sound advice. Thank you Mom, Sandi, Karen, Jan, and Diane.

A special thank you to all family and friends for their support and enthusiasm.

And finally, I would like to thank my husband and my son for their unfailing support and encouragement through this exciting experience.

A thought I wrote down on March 28, 1995:

> Things seem to make a hell of a lot more sense when you sit back and just let things happen. Some of the most important things in your life seem to just fall into place when you least expect it. This seems to make life worth living; you even start to think that maybe some of your wishes aren't just wishes after all. For without the dreamer there is no dream, without the dream there is no motivation.

About the Author

Thank you for taking your time to read *Forever Italy*. I was inspired to write this book while pregnant with my son. He was born with severe special needs and Goldenhar syndrome. I decided when he was six months old that I needed to fulfill my own dreams no matter what happens. This book was written during a lot of hospital stays that are ongoing; it's a wonderful outlet that takes me away from my present circumstances. The lesson that I have learned so far in his young life (almost two years old now) is to never give up hope and to always follow your heart.

FOREVER ITALY

1

Sidney Hamilton looked out the window of her New York apartment, watching the pounding rain trickling down the windowpane; the sky looked mad and dark as lightning streaked across the sky. Sidney, just out of a delicious bubble bath, tightened her terry cloth robe and, reaching under the collar, released her long red wavy hair. Sidney liked storms; they reminded her of her past—rocky and character building, captivating in the strength of its sometimes fearful grip on her. Sidney was a mature, tough twenty-six-year-old. Life had been anything but kind to her. Her parents were killed in a freak skiing accident when she was twelve. It had been unusually warm that year, which had caused the avalanche that buried her parents alive. By the time the rescue party reached them, they had suffocated to death. It taught Sidney that life wasn't fair. Part of her died that day with them; she no longer felt like a child.

She was then thrust into the care of her aunt Thelma in New York. Thelma owned a hair salon on Boston Avenue. The salon did fairly well, making them enough money for Sidney to enter into college and then go on to university. Sidney excelled in her scholastics; failure was not acceptable to her. She achieved her degree in marketing. Before she knew it, she was working for an established marketing firm in her home state. It was a perfect position.

She was traveling across the country promoting their latest product, the iPod XLT. A tool that she too would be hard-pressed to live without. She'd been on the road and planes now for at least five states; she'd begun to lose count and had to admit that she was feeling quite tired. The last two weeks had taken their toll on her body and her mind. She had her presentations down pat—she swore she was reciting them in her sleep. The last two years had been financially rewarding, affording her an adequate lifestyle, apartment, and vehicle. Sidney was strong, too strong sometimes for her own good. She hadn't taken a break in the last two years, and it was starting to show.

After debriefing with her boss that afternoon, he'd asked to speak with her privately in his office.

As she claimed the distance between the doorway and the open chair in front of her, Sidney questioned her subconscious as to what she'd done wrong.

Once seated, he'd commented on how hard she had been working; Sidney pressed on when others would have taken at least three weeks holiday by now. "I love what I do, Mr. Warner. I know I'm looking a little tired, but I still have some gas in the tank."

"I know you do, Sidney, but I strongly feel that you would benefit greatly if you had a real holiday. I want you to take at least a month off to recharge your batteries. Your one of our top sellers, and I can't have you burning out on me. The company needs you. I should have insisted the last two years when you refused to take your holidays."

Sidney tilted her head up higher. "If you're insisting on this, OK. But don't expect me to enjoy myself. I live to work. I swear I'm working in my dreams sometimes, thinking of the next great commercial idea or billboard feature. I'll leave at the end of the week. That gives me four days to figure out just where exactly I'm going to go."

Mr. Warner smiled. "I'm pleased at how easily you've taken my suggestion. You're great at what you do here. Go, have a wonderful time and let that beautiful hair of yours down. It's life that's waiting out there for you."

Sidney closed the drapes, shutting out the murky night. Wearing her fluffy blue slippers, she padded into the kitchen to put the kettle on for a cup of tea. She'd ordered pizza for dinner earlier and then had her nice bubble bath. She filled the copper chinese teapot up with boiled water and steeped her chamomile tea bag. "Now to figure out where I want to vacation." Sidney sighed and wondered what in the devil she was headed for, who she would meet, and what adventures lay ahead. Sidney had some male relationships, but whenever things got too complicated or too involved, Sidney shut down and ran the other way—or they did. It wasn't that she didn't like men or want a future with one, she was afraid to love. And the truth was, she just hadn't met a man who could override her own fear of loss. She had loved her parents with all her heart, had so many tender memories of Christmas and birthdays together that it was hard for her to trust her heart. She loved her aunt Thelma dearly, but that too had taken time. Her aunt had borne such a strong resemblance to her mother that Sidney would just look at her aunt and be reminded of what she had lost in her mom. Aunt Thelma had done the very best that she could, to do right by her niece, and Sadie loved her for it.

Sidney poured her tea and headed into her living room to browse the Internet and the travel magazines she'd picked up on her way home from the office. Setting down her tea, she got comfortable on her oversized couch; she had a feeling she was going to be there awhile. "I could go to Africa on a safari, an Alaskan cruise to see the icebergs, or Disneyland to meet Donald Duck. Mmm, so many choices." Sidney spent two hours entrenched in all the information online and in the catalogues. When her eyelids kept sliding down of their own accord, she knew it was time for bed. Vowing to reengage the quest tomorrow night, she shut her laptop and went to crawl into bed. As she closed her eyes, she listened to the sound of the rain pattering against the window.

In her dreams that night, she saw blue water with mists of cloud vapor rising up to the cliffs where she was standing atop of. The warm breeze wiped at her long red hair. Behind her, she swore she heard a voice calling her name as if drifting up to her on the wind and whispering her name in her ear.

The week went on in the usual humdrum of business while she worked at the office. Tying up loose ends with clients and making sure that all was well with confirmed marketing clients for the near future. Jackie, her assistant, was very capable of handling the rest of her accounts until she returned from her trip. But Sidney being organized and thorough wanted to make life with her gone as easy as possible.

On Wednesday night Aunt Thelma came over for supper like she normally did when her niece was in town. They had such a strong bond. They were all each other had except for a few close friends. "So how's the salon doing, busy as usual I hope?" Sidney asked as she poured water into a pot to boil for their spaghetti noodles.

"Oh, you know . . . it's wonderful. The other stylists are so busy too. I'm thinking of opening another shop on the other side of town. I really believe it could be a success given enough time, energy, and of course, money. Mind you, I'd have to cut down on my regular days to maybe two a week in order to run the other shop productively. Perhaps I'll hire an assistant manager to watch over business while I'm away at the new shop. But I think it could work." Aunt Thelma rested her head in her hand and traced her finger along Sidney's counter, engrossed in her own thoughts.

Sidney smiled, "Knowing you, I believe you'll do it too. You're a determined woman and usually get what you go after. Congrats on the idea. Speaking of getting what you go after . . . how's Maurice these days?"

From her perch on the bar stool, it was now Aunt Thelma's turn to smile as she looked down into her glass, swirling it within her grasp. "I have to tell you, it's going quite well. He makes me feel sixteen again. I really love being with him." Maurice and Aunt Thelma had met at his bakery on twenty-fourth where Aunt Thelma picked up her buns, breads, and desserts. Three months had gone by before Maurice had enough courage to ask Thelma out for coffee.

Maurice was a widower of ten years. His wife had died of a sudden and fatal heart attack. The death of his wife had shocked Maurice to his core. His young children, Cora and Luke, had only been eleven at the time of their mother's death. Life had gone on, and like many widowed families, Maurice had many challenges of being both mother and father to the twins. All in all, Maurice was very proud of the young adults his children had become. Cora had become an airline stewardess, and Luke was in school to become a dentist. His children had encouraged him to date, saying that he needed to think of his own happiness, and wouldn't life be more exciting when he could share it with someone?

Now that his children were older and out exploring their own lives, he decided to at least be open to the idea. Not even two weeks later, Thelma Cooper walked into his bakery and also into his heart. Her eyes sparkled of life and with a depth hard to describe. He was instantly drawn to her. Even so, it had been so long since he'd been on the dating scene. He wondered if things still worked the same way. Had the rules changed over time? Not knowing what to do, he'd waited to see some sign from her that she was even interested in him. Would she linger just a fraction of a second longer than necessary or wink? He didn't know. They were the oldest signs of attraction in the book. And one day, he saw the wink and the lingering pause all in the same visit to the bakery. The very next time he saw her, he mustered all his courage and asked her out. She didn't seem at all surprised by the question, and smiling into his green eyes, she said she'd love to. Now months later both felt like they were in love.

Sidney poured some oil and salt into the water and stared at her aunt who was still looking dreamily into her wine. "I'm so happy for you. It's nice to see you excited about life and all the adventures you have ahead." Thelma looked at her niece. "Talking about adventures, why don't we try to figure out where you're going. Do you have any ideas?"

Sidney shrugged. "I've got a couple of places in mind, but I'd like to go over some of them with you."

Thelma laughed. "I don't know how much help I'll be. I haven't really been to a lot of places, but with the help of the Internet, it shouldn't be too hard to look at some hotels and hot spots. What kind of trip are you looking for? A fiesta of activities or just parking your tush on a beach somewhere and having piña coladas served to you via a handsome cabana boy in a Speedo?" After the mental picture and their laughter subsided, they moved to the kitchen table waiting for the noodles, sauce, and garlic toast to finish cooking. "How about Australia?" Aunt Thelma suggested. "I've heard that it's a nice place to visit."

"It's a possibility, but I'm looking for a place full of romance and very exotic," Sidney said softly as though lost in thought.

"You should go to Italy," Aunt Thelma said excitedly.

"I'd love to research it, though I have to admit just the name makes goose bumps rise on my arms. Look . . ." Sure enough Sidney did have goose bumps.

After dinner, they both got comfy on the couch and typed *Italy* into the search engine. Before they knew it, they were looking at hotels, tourist destinations, points of interest, and festival events. Sidney was getting more excited every moment they researched. They looked at a couple of other destinations just for the heck of it, but Sidney already knew in her heart of hearts that she just had to go to Italy.

After their strawberry shortcake dessert, the two embraced and talked of making plans with Maurice and the twins to get together upon her return home from her trip. They both agreed it would be wonderful for all to meet as it looked like Maurice was going to be a fixture in both their lives.

They said goodnight, and when Sidney shut the door, she leaned against it and sighed the word *Italy* softly on her lips. She fell asleep that night, giddy with happiness and a sense of excitement in her heart.

She booked her trip on Thursday and was thinking about it all the way to work on Friday. When she approached her desk, she saw the flowers: stargazer lilies, white carnations, and a card. She opened the card and saw the Italian money inside; the card read:

Dear Sidney,

    Take this money and spend it pampering yourself, perhaps a massage at your hotel. Have a great vacation, you've definitely earned it.

                                                 Yours Truly,
                                                       Jackie

Sidney was truly touched at her assistant's thoughtfulness. She turned around, and there was Jackie bringing her her coffee. "Thank you so very much, I can't believe this is really happening."

Jackie laughed. "I'm sure it will all become very real once you've landed on the tarmac. Remember to call me if you need anything professionally or personally." They both embraced, and Sidney thanked her again, thinking how lucky she was to have such a great assistant and friend.

Sidney left that day at noon to go shopping for her trip, saying goodbye to everyone on her way out. Her flight left at four thirty on Monday morning, so the countdown was on. She really needed some summer clothes that were not presentable for the office. At least living in the Great Apple afforded her with many shops to choose from. Sidney kept up with the latest fashion trends, so it was a great feeling to walk into the stores and know what she was looking for.

In the first three shops, she purchased lightweight and sexy V-neck tank tops with an added strip of lace fabric below the bust line for an added flare. She got them in complimentary colors to her hair and green eyes. She also bought some shorts, a couple of skirts, and a white wrap to wear on the breezier days and nights. She saved the most important garment for last, the almighty bikini.

She went to a specialty store for this. After trying on about eight different styles, she finally settled on a white bikini with pastel traces of green and aqua blue. It hugged her in all the right places. Thank god for her workout schedule and a belief that no matter how busy her life was she'd always make time to work out at least twice a week even if that only meant going for a run around the hotel she was staying in.

She was five feet six inches tall and was all leg, a fact that her male coworkers seemed to notice. Sidney knew there was the potential of meeting someone, but she didn't want to complicate her life, so she was going on her vacation with the thought of just relaxing her mind and spirit. Sidney had a hard time keeping men; it wasn't that she was a hermit, just that she simply was never in town long enough to give all the time and attention to them. In the end they would always complain and lose interest in her, leaving her for someone who did have the time. Due in part to this, Sidney had a hard time opening up to men, never giving her full heart knowing that they too would eventually leave. No, Sidney was only going for a vacation. At times she could have a thick outer shell and could be hard to read. She only hoped that the Italian men would be able to tell this about her at first sight and leave her be.

Sidney left the shops happily with her parcels. She knew she would probably buy more clothes once she got to Italy.

When she arrived home, she saw the light flashing on her answering machine. The message was urgent—to please call her aunt's place immediately when she got home. Feeling a little alarmed, Sidney called her right away.

"Aunt Thelma . . . what's happened?"

"It's not Aunt Thelma, Sidney. It's Luke. Your aunt has been in a car accident, and she's in the hospital. I'm not sure what her injuries are. The hospital called my dad when you couldn't be reached." Sidney had let her cell phone die out as she hadn't intended on bringing it while she was on vacation. "Oh my god! What hospital is she in?" Sidney asked frantically.

"She's in Cedar Green. Listen, Sidney, take a cab down there. I don't want you driving. I'll meet you outside the main entrance, and then I'll take you back home later," Luke said very quickly.

"OK . . . and, Luke, thank you. I'll see you there." Though they had never met, Sidney already knew they would get along. Sidney called the first cab company in the yellow pages and raced downstairs to await the cab. All sorts of horrible things ran through her mind. Tears streaked down her face, yet Sidney barely noticed. Her aunt meant everything to her. She was the only family that she had since her parents' death, which still felt like yesterday. She couldn't stand the thought of losing her aunt too. The memories of her parents' untimely exit of this world were still very close to the surface of her heart no matter how much time had passed.

Sidney reached the hospital fifteen minutes later. As she got out of the cab, a tall handsome young man queried, "Sidney?" He reached out his hand. "Yes." She reached out her own hand and shook his. He then dug into his pocket and offered her a Kleenex. Luke looked at her flushed cheeks and said, "This way . . ." They walked into the hospital and over to the emergency room desk and asked for Thelma Cooper.

"Right this way please." Sidney could read no expression on the nurse's face. She escorted them over to one of the many curtained partitions and pulled back the curtain on number twelve.

There lay her aunt with Maurice at her bedside. He moved over the minute he saw Sidney. Thelma looked up at her niece and smiled. "Oh, I'm sorry to have worried everyone so! I'm fine, really, just a big bump on the forehead from the steering wheel." Thelma went on with the story. "This jerk wasn't looking where he was going and banged right into the back of my car. I must have lost consciousness because the next thing I knew, I was in the ambulance heading for here."

During her aunt's explanation, Sidney had rushed to her bedside, kissed her on the cheek and sat next to Maurice, and clasped her hand in her own lap. The tears came cascading down her cheeks again but this time with relief and love for her aunt.

"It's OK, dear," her aunt said, trying to be reassuring. She reached up to stroke her temple and then the cheek of the only daughterlike niece she'd ever known. And then she too was in tears. Sidney managed to whisper between choked emotion, "I thought I was going to lose you too. I was so scared."

Aunt Thelma said, "It'd take a lot more than that to get rid of me. I'm not going anywhere. I plan to be around for a very long time yet, so don't you worry!" By now they had almost dried all their tears. Sidney looked at Maurice, leaned over, and hugged the man that brought her aunt so much happiness. "Thank you, Maurice, for being here for my aunt." Maurice genuinely returned the hug.

Just then they heard a gentle clearing of a throat. "Hi, Dad. Hello, Ms. Cooper." Maurice looked up and introduced Cora to Sidney. Luke was still standing behind his father watching the raw emotions being exchanged and was relieved himself that Ms. Cooper would be all right. Sidney got up to stand beside Luke so that Maurice could be next to Aunt Thelma. He embraced her hands and looked adoringly at her. Aunt Thelma started to chuckle. "I never dreamed that we would all meet in such circumstances."

Maurice cleared his throat. "And I never dreamed that I would be proposing in such circumstances. I was setting up a whole 'to-do' for this evening, but I just can't wait any longer. Almost losing you . . . I just can't bear the thought of waiting one more second. Thelma Cooper, I love you with all of my soul. The last four months have been amazing, and I love you more with every passing day. I know that life is now. Will you marry me?" The tears started again as

Maurice—still holding Thelma's hands, IV and all—bent down on one knee on the hospital floor and asked for Thelma Cooper's hand in marriage.

"YES! Absolutely!" Thelma said as the tears streamed down her cheeks. When the doctor came in a few minutes later, they were all in tears and embracing one another in their happiness. Even Luke couldn't hide his wet eyes.

"I swear she's going to be all right," the doctor said earnestly. Once Thelma filled him in, the doctor expressed sincere congratulations to the happy new family.

A little later on, when in private with her aunt, Sidney asked, "Are you sure you're going to be OK without me for a month? Maybe this was a sign not to go?"

Thelma answered while shaking her head. "I believe, my dear, that it is your destiny to go. You need to take a break, rest your beautiful mind, and nourish your soul. We'll start planning the wedding when you get back. Maurice and I want to get married in the spring, so there's at least three months for us. We have time. I want you to go. Besides you've got lots of souvenirs to bring back for me."

Sidney embraced her aunt for the last time. "I love you, Aunt Thelma. I'll call you when I can."

"I love you too, sweetheart. Now go and have a wonderful adventure . . ."

2

It was still pitch-dark when Sidney's alarm clock went off at 3:00 a.m. After her twenty-minute shower, she quickly dressed in the layered outfit that she had previously set out for herself the night before. She quickly called a cab and, for the second time that day, waited for it to arrive downstairs. It came quickly, and she hurried into its interior. As luck would have it, the predicted rain had begun to fall. *I'm so glad to leave this weather behind*, Sidney thought to herself. Once seated comfortably in her waiting area within the warmth of the airport, she waited for her flight to be called. To her surprise, there were quite a few people heading to Italy. She always wondered where people were going. Were they tourists like her, or were they going back to their native country? Sidney knew she'd never know, but she still couldn't help her curiosity.

Sidney packed her usual travel tools that helped her get through the flight. Even though she traveled a lot and should've been used to flying by now, she really didn't like it at all. For one, she had an honest-to-God fear of heights; second of all, she had motion sickness; and third, she almost always got stuck next to the person that wanted to talk her ear off the entire flight. Talk about a great recipe for disaster.

Sidney was in luck she had the aisle seat. Which meant she wouldn't be able to see how high up she was, and her long legs would be able to inhabit the aisleway whenever possible.

Sidney had just packed all her carry-on belongings in the overhead compartment and was relaxing in her seat. She closed her eyes and felt excitement course through her veins, a smile instantaneously washed across her face. Her journey had begun.

"Excuse me, I believe that I have the seat next to you," a masculine voice said.

Oh boy, here we go, Sidney thought to herself. Then she opened her eyes, and what stared back at her were the most gorgeous green eyes she'd ever seen before in her life, except her own of course.

"Oh . . . sure, just let me get up so you can get in," Sidney said as she moved to get out of her seat. He moved past her and sat down.

"My name is Marcos, pleased to meet you." Marcos held out his hand. Sidney extended hers and was surprised by the warmth she felt.

"My name's Sidney. It's nice to meet you too." Sidney felt a warm flush wash across her face before releasing his hand. Embarrassed, she ducked her head down and pretended to smooth out her pants.

What's wrong with me? She angrily mentally checked herself. Marcos looked Italian. His striking eyes were complemented by a square strong jaw, perfectly set cheekbones, short brown nicely cut hair, and long eyelashes.

Marcos was silently taking Sidney in as well. He loved her hair, so radiant against her pale skin. She had beautiful hands. He saw her blush at their earlier touch, and it piqued his curiosity. He wanted to know a lot more about this attractive lady.

"Are you traveling alone, Sidney?" Marcos asked as he buckled his seat belt.

Sidney wondered just what kind of question that was and started to become a little leery of her neighbor. "Um . . . ," Sidney hesitated.

"Oh, I know that came out entirely wrong. Sorry. What I meant to ask is, are you traveling on vacation?" Sidney, still feeling a little put off, was vague in her response. "Yes." Dead silence. Marcos knew without a doubt that he'd really stuck his foot in it. He decided to try a new route and started talking about himself instead in an attempt to help her relax and realize he wasn't a total creep.

"I love Italy. It's where I come from. My family owns a vineyard, which I am going to inherit one day. It's just amazing. I love watching the sun dipping gently across the waving hillside, and the sun is this orange rust color with sweeps of purple," Marcos said. As Sidney watched him talk of his vineyard, she thought he had totally lost his mind. She knew that Italian men were romantic, but this was the stuff out of some romance novel!

He had passion. She had to give him that. Too many unhappy people had lost this wonderful quality in their lives, and it left them feeling unfulfilled. Something she knew she never wanted to feel, yet she had to admit, sometimes did. She had passion for her work, and she was proud of everything that she had accomplished in her life. Though sporadically when she came home to her lonely apartment, she felt all too aware that passion in other aspects of her life was certainly not apparent. In that instant, she realized that she might learn a thing or two from this sexy Italian and decided to give him a chance.

Just then, the preflight information was done. "Let's hope we won't need any of that!" Marcos said, half laughing.

Sidney took a deep breath and blew it out slowly. "No kidding," Sidney replied as she reached for her seat belt and grabbed on to it reassuringly. The engine started to get louder as the pilots did their preflight testing before takeoff. They watched as the wing flaps moved up and down.

"Are you OK? You seem a little nervous," Marcos commented.

"I'll be all right once we hit the tarmac in Italy. I fly a lot for my work, but it doesn't stop me from getting a little anxious especially with the takeoff and landing," Sidney said, taking another deep breath in. The palms of her hands were starting to sweat now.

"Are you a control freak or something? Lots of people are afraid of flying because they have no control over their surroundings."

Sidney turned wide-eyes on him and was understandably taken aback. "Are you kidding me! You've known me for five minutes, and you've already asked me two completely insane questions," Sidney retorted. "And just for the record, no, I am not a control freak. I am, however, afraid of heights and have a habit of getting sick. I sure hope that for the rest of the trip that you consider what you're going to say to me, or don't bother at all!" Sidney was trying to control her temper. Marcos sure could get under her skin, and she was beginning to see that her neighbor was not only just as bad as the usual "talkers" she had labeled and barely tolerated; he was simply worse for insulting her with his lame brain, unchecked idea of conversation.

This is going to be a long flight, she thought to herself.

And then she heard the *ding* of the seat belt sign go off allowing the passengers to move freely about the cabin. She couldn't believe it. They were already at their cruising altitude.

She looked over at Marcos who was grinning at her from ear to ear. "I knew that would get you through it." Sidney gawked at him, her mouth moving, but it took her a moment to register what he had done for her.

"You mean you just said the control freak question to get my mind off the takeoff?" Sidney asked.

"Yes," Marcos confirmed, triumphantly smiling at her. Sidney looked into his green eyes just a little harder. "Thank you. I'm sorry that I was so mean to you. You were just trying to help me." Sidney looked down into her lap feeling a bit embarrassed, grateful, and still a little put off.

Marcos put his finger gently under her chin, turning her face toward him, and said, "You're too beautiful to waste time feeling bad. So don't. Apology accepted and you're welcome. It was my pleasure." Sidney continued to drown in his eyes for a moment longer and then broke away when the stewardess came by to take their drink order. The captain came on and told them of the movie selections for their trip, *Wall-E* and *Front Living*. One was the latest movie released, and she was excited to watch them.

They had a six-hour flight ahead of them. Both were happy that they were sitting with someone that they could at least tolerate. Of course, it was more than that. What Sidney didn't know was she was sitting beside the man of one of the most affluent families in Italy. Not only did they owned a winery, they owned a good portion of the Italian wine market. Their wine was the best,

Cortina d'Ampezzo, after the Italian Alps that watered their vines with its rich purity. The wine was known for its full body reds and lighter-than-clouds white wine. Marcos thought it best to leave his true identity unspoken. He was used to people only wanting to associate with him because of his last name and what they could get out of a friendship with him; it was why he went to New York on a much-needed holiday. He had been gone for two months. He had met some college students on the Internet, kept his true identity hidden as he usually did, and hung out with them as they hit the local bars. He went to the museum and did a lot of shopping for his sisters. He had three. They had given Marcos a long shopping list of knickknacks and clothing must-haves that were not available in Italy.

He met other people as well. Samantha. Thinking of her name brought a smile to his full lips. She was a bartender at one of the local pubs close to the hotel he'd been staying at. He had gone there pretty regularly, and they had struck up a friendship. She was working at the pub during the night and working on her college degree during the day. She wanted to be a psychologist and was at the end of her fourth year. The day she had finished, they had both gone out and gotten stinking drunk. Before they knew it, they were back in Marcos's hotel room stripping off their clothing while their lips were locked together. Even though he was drunk, Marcos was a true Italian and took his time pleasing her; she was not disappointed.

The next morning they realized what had happened and were stunned at their lack of responsibility. They hadn't used protection. Samantha assured him that she would take care of it, although she was sure that everything was fine since she had just had her monthly friend. They both knew that they would remain friends and only friends. Besides, he was leaving next week, and neither wanted to get too attached. They had dinner together the night before he left. When he dropped her at her door later that evening, they embraced and laughed, promising to write and not lose contact. And they meant it. Samantha had a special quality about her. She seemed genuinely interested in people and wanted to help them with life's pitfalls. Marcos had seen a lot of uncaring people in his twenty-seven years on the planet. He knew he wouldn't forget her.

The flight went smoothly with only a couple of bumps from turbulence. Sidney and Marcos enjoyed watching the movies, especially *Front Living*. A half hour before landing, Marcos asked, "I would love to see you more. Would that be all right?"

Sidney took a breath and looked down at her lap before answering. "I'm really flattered, and I think you're a nice-enough guy. I just don't think that I'm ready to start anything while I'm away on vacation. I just don't think it's smart. Sorry." Sidney smiled at Marcos trying to take any hurt away that her words might have caused. She was drawn to Marcos and could see herself falling for him. They'd only been together six hours, but she already felt a connection forming between them. Obviously, he did too.

He returned her smile. "I only meant that we should have some drinks some time. I usually don't move too fast with any relationship. I'm sorry if I gave you the wrong impression."

Sidney turned a nice shade of pink. "Oh. Well, in that case, I would like that very much. Maybe I'll run into you on my trip at one of the local piazzas." Marcos smiled back at her. Before they knew it, the plane was touching down in Italy. Sidney was excited, and Marcos laughed at her giddiness.

After getting off the plane and collecting their luggage, he walked her outside to collect a taxi for her. When the cab came, she turned to him awkwardly. In his thick accent, he said, "Goodbye, Sidney," and leaned in and kissed her on both her cheeks as was the custom.

Sidney knew it was traditional and tried to not be affected by his unexpected contact but couldn't help her hand from reaching up and caressing her own flaming cheek. "I guess I'll have to get used to that. I hope to see you again, Marcos." With that, she stepped into the cab and waved to him as the cab moved into the traffic.

Wow! she thought to herself. If all the men were this charming, she knew she was in for one hell of a vacation!

FOREVER ITALY

3

Once they were away from the airport and the city surrounding it, Sidney was able to see the true beauty of the country. Large sprawling vineyards dotted the landscape of soft and sharp contrasting hillside landscapes. She absolutely adored the palm trees that seemed to come out of nowhere. The cypress trees were tall enough to build a tree fort in. It reminded her that she was a long way from home. She didn't think that she could be any more excited until the moment she saw the ocean as they rounded a cliffside curve. The blueness of the water was breathtaking, and she couldn't think of any where else she'd want to be.

All her life she had strived to be the best at everything. This attitude had gotten her to where she wanted to be, but it came with a high cost, relaxation. She could not honestly remember the last time that she had truly felt relaxed. She had a feeling that this month-long trip would afford her the freedom to do just that. As they drove farther along the coast, the driver, who spoke English well, pointed at the large volcanic rock formations and explained the likeness to animals and persons of interest.

They had been on the road for an hour when she first spotted the little town of Riomaggiore. She had researched all the spots that she would be staying at and knew a few distinguishing markings. It was a magical-looking city, nestled in the cliffside. As the sun shone on the buildings, the colors coming off were pinkish white and caramel cream. She decided it looked delicious enough to eat and laughed to herself.

The taxi drew up to the front entrance of her hotel. There were large blue, red, and yellow flowers growing semiwildly in terra-cotta pots all around the front of the building. She loved flowers but unfortunately was never home long enough to grow her own. The ones she purchased usually died before she could get home from her trips to water them.

She looked at the tall white building. It was old, three stories high with wrought iron balconies coming off Italian glass doors. There was just enough ivy crawling up the sides of the building to finish off this classic look. To Sidney it was a picture-perfect postcard.

She breathed in the warm clean air and smiled to herself thinking, *Finally. I think I'm beginning to relax or what I imagine relaxing to feel like.* Sidney picked up her bags and walked into the welcoming piazza. A lady dressed in a flowing red and blue flowered dress with a golden tan smiled at her from behind the front desk. "Hello, signora. You have come to stay with us . . . yes?"

Sidney put down her bags and happily replied, "Yes. You have such a beautiful place here. I'll be here for one week. I believe you'll find me under Hamilton."

The lady introduced herself. "My name is signora Chiara. This is my hotel, and you may come to me if you require anything beyond what my caretakers can provide you. I believe that you will love your stay here. It is the most beautiful town on this stretch of coast. It has been my home for ten years, and I know I wouldn't be able to live anywhere else now that I have been infected with the beauty of this now peaceful land. Here is your room key, and Theo will show you to your room. Ciao, signora Sidney." Sidney wondered what had put the happy glint of light in the woman's eyes. Now knowing that it had been this wonderful place, Sidney knew that she too was ready to be so inspired.

Theo picked up her bags and walked toward a worn marble staircase that wound spiraling up to the second and third floors. Theo was a middle-aged man of medium build and a dusting of a few grey hairs that added maturity to his face. He too also seemed to always be smiling. He chatted with her briefly about where she was from and what area of business she was in. He seemed to be interested in her area of work and seemed to want to know more. Before they were too engrossed in this conversation, they were at her door. Theo put her bags down, biding her farewell. Sidney smiled and said she'd love to meet him for a drink the next day once she had settled in.

She put her old key in its lock and turned the knob gently, pushing the door open. Her room was a wash of cream and white colors with accents of blue. Green plants with budding flowers hung on shelves on each wall. Soft white flowing curtains moved to the breeze coming from beyond. Sidney moved toward the queen-size bed. Setting her belongings down, she jumped on the bed with an exuberant squeal of delight and lay there on her back enjoying the moment. She closed her eyes and thought of all the things that were ahead for her. She was overcome with emotion and the feeling of sudden release and freedom.

She looked beyond the edge of the bed and saw a bathroom with a claw-foot bathtub, shower, sink, and toilet. Pretty standard although the bathtub was a bonus she hadn't expected. She looked to her right and again looked at the billowing curtains. Curious, she got off the bed and gingerly pulled one of the curtains back. What she saw took her breath away. In front of her was a wrought iron terrace with baskets of beautiful flowers hanging in pots off the rail. However, this is not what took her breath away. It was the gorgeous ocean view.

Sadie took off her shoes and walked onto the warm balcony. Leaning over the rail, she watched the waves crashing below her onto the beautiful soft white sand beach. The delicious blue ocean was a sight she knew she wouldn't forget any time soon. She looked over to the left where there was a very nice lounge chair awaiting her butt, which she eagerly sank into. As she lay in the lounger, she watched the waves crest and then break on one another before completely ridding themselves onto the sandy beach. Sidney had never felt so happy in her whole life.

Now in this space of time, she truly was free. She had no attachments, no bills, and no one depending on her except herself. She knew that this was possibly the only time in her life that things would be like this and knew that not taking full advantage would be a waste and a sin.

She went back inside to put on her bikini and noticed that on top of the dresser to the left was a bottle of white wine chilling in a bucket of ice with two wineglasses and an opener. After she put on her suit, she busied herself with opening it. The label was Cortina d'Ampezzo. She'd never heard of them. *Probably a small local vineyard*, Sidney thought to herself. She poured her glass full, grabbed the bottle, and stepped out onto her terrace and watched the waves; the sound of them was so rhythmical that two and a half glasses later, she fell asleep in the lounge chair. Her dreams were pure relaxation; everything was light and floating. She awoke to the sun setting. The sky was magical with colors of blue, purple, and pink, all falling into one another. A half hour later as night descended, she was in awe at how many stars there were in the sky, so big and so close. She'd never seen anything nearly this beautiful at home. She felt lighthearted and happy.

She reveled in these sensations as she went back inside, turning on the bedroom lights. Going to her suitcase, she pulled out one of her dresses and the light white wrap she had brought just in case it got breezy. Deciding it was time for her to eat, she headed out of her room and down the stairs to eat at the hotel restaurant. Once she was down the spiral staircase, she followed the signs. Theo, the caretaker who had showed her to her room earlier, smiled warmly as he showed her to a table. Sidney couldn't believe her eyes. Outside, everything was white linen and candles. There were strings of lights in the trees all around, white sashes hung on their branches as they billowed in the caressing wind. Below her, Sidney could hear the waves as they skimmed up the sandy beach. She felt as if she was in a different world, a very surreal dream at best. Sidney looked around her with wide eyes and just smiled to herself. Never before had she felt so far away from everything, and she felt a feeling of such sweet contentment.

There were only a handful of people at the restaurant, most of them couples. Theo brought her a menu and asked what she would like to drink. She asked for a glass of the brand of wine that had been left in her room. Theo smiled and went to retrieve the beverage.

Sidney pondered the menu and decided on the most traditional Italian dish that she was aware of and ordered the spaghetti and meatballs. She also ordered another two glasses of the delicious white wine. Her meal was everything and then some, filling her up to the brim that she desperately needed, considering the amount of wine that she'd consumed in the last couple of hours. Still working on her last glass of wine, she felt slightly giddy and was just starting to get up and leave when she heard a voice behind her.

"Leaving so soon? Why don't you have one more glass of wine and keep me company?"

Sidney turned around and looked at the handsome stranger and shrugged her shoulders. "Normally I wouldn't just sit down with a stranger, but since I'm on holiday, why not?"

He was two tables over from her, and Sidney moved almost normally over to an awaiting chair. She was feeling her liquid courage course through her veins. She smiled at him before sitting, extended her hand and introduced herself. He clasped her hand and leaned forward as he kissed the top, saying, "It is all my pleasure. My name is Tonio. Please, have a seat. I hate to eat alone, but due to my present circumstances, it may be a good possibility throughout my trip." Tonio picked up his glass of wine and swirled it around looking thoughtful.

Sidney looked at him perplexed. "I don't know how you could feel lonely with this surreal beauty all around you."

Sidney felt like she was glowing, and it wasn't just from the wine.

"It is because of the beauty that I feel ill-content. You see, my dear, I am on my honeymoon right now." Sidney gasped and started to apologize while she started to rise from her chair.

"Hold on a moment, it's not what it seems. Please let me explain." Sidney sat down in her chair. "Her name was Angelica. We had been dating for several years, and I thought I knew everything about her. I should have seen the writing on the wall. No woman in the world could've had that many facials. It turns out that the only thing being buffed wasn't her face. She told me the day of our supposed wedding. She suddenly had an attack of conscience and said she simply couldn't marry me. She'd been cheating on me for quite some time. I couldn't believe it. I couldn't even say anything to her for I knew that no words would be able to convey my deepest hurt and anger. I turned my back on her and walked out onto the street and into the nearest cab. I haven't talked to her since, and I doubt that I ever will again. I feel so foolish for not seeing the signs."

Sidney felt at a loss for words. What really could you say to a person who had just had their heart crushed? She knew that she had to try for his sake.

"It's hard to understand. I only know that you have to be extremely careful of who you let in," Sidney said gently. "I believe you have to hope that all interests are well placed. Doing it and saying it are two different things though, and I too have a problem with that." Trying to change the subject to a lighter tone, she asked, "How long are you staying here?" Sidney sipped at her wine.

Tonio grimaced. "Two weeks and I have no idea of what to do with myself." Trying for lightness that he himself didn't feel, he joked, "I'm sure that my tan will get much darker and my swimming skills will improve. How about you, what's your story?"

Sidney smiled into her wine. "Well, I'm actually on vacation for the first time in as long as I can remember." Sidney tucked her blowing hair behind her ear. "I love it here. It's everything that I could wish for." As she said it, her gaze went out and up to the lovely stars.

"What do you do for your living, Sidney, or should I guess?" Tonio asked.

"Well, I'm in advertising. I travel across the States doing one presentation after the next. I love what I do, and this trip is my reward," Sidney stated. "What do you do?" she countered back, smiling.

"I'm a travel agent by day and a writer at night. I guess it's my romantic side shining through. I write short poems, have a weekly column in the local paper. But my day job is as a travel agent."

Sidney started to laugh. Then she remembered their present states of alcohol-induced conversation and quickly covered her laughter with a cough. "Well, that sounds very interesting. You must know all the hot spots here in Italy, then?"

"Yes, you could say that." Tonio smiled at her. He found her very attractive, and he liked what he saw when she stood up to come sit at his table. He was still a man after all and appreciated women taking care of themselves. "I could show you around this part of the city if and when you wanted. And you know that I'm harmless. After what I've been through, I need a good long break before I think romantically about someone." Tonio downed the rest of his wine, adding emphasis to his statement.

Sydney felt truly sad for him. He seemed decent enough. Sydney could honestly say that she thought his now ex was an absolute bitch. What Angelica had done to Tonio was inconceivable to Sidney. She just hoped he wasn't permanently scarred. One never knows when the love of your life is going to walk in.

Sydney felt a sudden urge to show him that not all women were insensitive and low. Deciding to take a chance, she accepted his offer. He told her of a hike and picnic tour that was running at ten the next morning. She agreed to meet him in the lobby and bid the lonely stranger good night.

The warm wind blew her dress cover gently against her knees. She felt so good. She rather liked having someone to pal around with. It was nice to have someone to talk to too, even if that meant that she might have to do some cheering up along the way. She enjoyed talking with him tonight even though they were a bit drunk. They already had three things in common: being alone, single, and liked to drink. These were not the greatest things to have in common, but she sensed a goodness in him that drew her curiously to him.

Sydney liked to sleep in the buff, and as she lay in bed that night, she drifted off to sleep to the sound of lullaby waves and the gentle wind billowing her curtains. Sydney smiled contently and let out a dreamy sigh.

4

Sydney met Tonio in the lobby at ten as discussed. He looked crisp and ready for the day, dressed in light shorts and a muscle shirt, which did justice to his strong arms. He had an impressive physique and obviously, like herself, made the time to take care of himself. Sydney dressed in light layers and had put on her hiking shoes. She didn't know what the terrain would be like and wanted to be sure not to hurt herself especially being at the beginning of her trip. They boarded the tour bus along with the rest of the vacationers from their hotel and headed off to their destination.

As their bus wound its way along the coastline, Tonio pointed out items of historic interest. When they rounded one curve, they came upon a large boulder that stuck out of the sea. Tonio said that it was known as the Love Rock and that all who gazed upon it could wish for their one true love and that he or she would come to them. Sydney laughed up into his smiling face. "That sounds very romantic, silly, and like an old wise tale to me. Yet what could it hurt? I think I will make a wish. You should try it too."

Sydney closed her eyes and made her wish. While she had her eyes closed, he too made his own wish, knowing that in fact it was an old wise tale and chuckled silently to himself.

They reached their destination of the Isla D'Ablo hiking trail. There was quite a bit of forest, and the ocean could be seen through little glimpses of the waving branches. The group of hikers was fifteen strong. The hike was not supposed to be hard. It was a relatively easy trail with only a couple of uneven terrain areas. Mike was their guide, and he went over the rules of no littering and no feeding the wildlife if they saw any.

They had been hiking on the easy part of the trail for about an hour. Sydney loved it! It was all so striking in its simplicity and beauty. She felt as free as the birds she heard chirping in the trees above her. Long had it been since she'd done anything like this. All her workouts had been at the gym. She realized with certain clarity that she must make an effort once she was home to get back to nature. She now realized how much she'd been missing. She felt this walk was actually feeding her soul, making her feel alive again in a way that she had never thought of acknowledging, all due in part to her being too busy with her career.

They reached a hilly area with some roots sticking out of the ground. Tonio passed in front of her. "Allow me to give you a hand please."

Tonio climbed up on top of the embankment and extended his hand down toward her. She looked up into his sincere eyes and, smiling at him, clasped his hand. He brought her up in one swift pull, straight into his arms. As their bodies collided, she felt the heat of his engulf her. Their hands still entwined, bodies compressed, she looked up into his startled eyes and felt a hot wave streak through her body and embarrassment.

"Oops" was all she could muster to say to Tonio. He covered his own reaction by clearing his throat as they untangled their bodies. She stepped around him and tried to make light of the situation by not responding further. She returned to walking in front of him and continued to hike up toward the others.

Tonio didn't want to think about their close contact in light of his current situation, but he had to admit that he'd liked being that close to her. He put it down to feeling comforted by another human being even if it was just a few seconds. She sure didn't seem that affected by it, so there was no harm done. Besides, he knew that he couldn't trust his feelings right now about anything or anyone. He needed time and a clear heart and head.

They were hiking to the top of the picnic site. Once they got there, they couldn't believe the view. It was gorgeous. As far as one could see, there were mountains and the immense ocean. The slight wind cooled their overheated bodies.

"Wow, that's quite the view," Sydney said to Tonio.

"Well worth the hike, wouldn't you say?" Tonio asked.

Remembering their bodies compressing, she replied, "Yes, I'd say so."

Sidney knew that she shouldn't have enjoyed the feeling of his hard body next to her so much. She couldn't help it though. She hardly knew him; he was almost a complete stranger. Spending an hour and a half with someone you got drunk with the night before hardly equaled a quality conversation. Yet it had been one of the best times in a long time. She was relaxed and didn't care so much about her presentation of herself to the point of being stressed out all the time. She felt loose. If that meant she wanted to feel something mild for a man who was emotionally off-limits, then why not. He would never know anyway; he wasn't even dating material right now for Pete's sakes.

The guide dug into his large packs and started to bring out their lunches of cold cut sandwiches, bottled water, and fruit onto the picnic tables. After Sydney and Tonio had dished out their food onto the paper plates, they sat down at a table with a young couple who, as they soon found out, were on their honeymoon.

Vanessa was tall and easy on the eyes while Jordan was a little shorter but had a huge smile that was very friendly.

"So where are you from?" Sydney asked.

Vanessa replied as Jordan had a mouth full of food. "We're from Toronto, Canada. Have you been there?"

"I've been there on a couple of business trips. Unfortunately, I usually don't have time to sightsee with my compressed schedule. Though it looks like a nice place to live. Tonio might have spent more time there. He's a travel agent," Sydney explained.

"Oh. I thought you two were together, my mistake." Vanessa took the opportunity to put her sandwich in her mouth.

Tonio shifted on his side of the bench. Smiling at the other couple, he said, "It's an easy assumption to make. We met at our hotel last night at dinner. We're both on our own for our holidays, so we decided to pal around together today. It's nice to have company, especially here." He didn't know why, but he felt the need to explain their situation.

Jordan spoke up. "Seems like fun to me. We're on our honeymoon. We really needed this after all the hectic planning of the wedding. So much stress for just one day. It was all worth it in the end. I would do anything for my sweetheart. I wouldn't have changed a thing." Jordan and Vanessa shared a long, loving, tender look that spoke volumes. It made Tonio feel like if they had been alone at that particular moment, they'd be making sweet love to one another right there on the spot. He suddenly felt nauseated.

Sydney cleared her throat, feeling slightly uncomfortable. She could tell that the situation was putting Tonio on edge. They chitchatted with the other couple lightly until their lunch was done. Sydney ate hers a little more quickly than she normally would as she had a plan to save the rest of the day for Tonio.

Seeing that he was working on his last bite, she said, "Well, thank you for the company. It was nice to meet you both. Tonio, I saw an artifact up the hill. Would you mind giving me a history lesson on it?"

Tonio, seeing the chance to escape the other couple, agreeably went with her toward the artifact. "Thanks. I appreciated that. I didn't know how much more I could handle. I'm glad that they're happy. I just wish that it didn't remind me of my own sadness."

Sensing his unhappiness before he even spoke, she reached across and touched his arm gently. "It's going to take some time, Tonio, but things will get better." She meant her touch to be a friendly gesture, and she hoped that he took it as such.

Tonio looked across at her and looked into her empathetic eyes. "I'm really sorry. I shouldn't be unloading this crap on you. You're on vacation, and I'm ruining it for you. That's not a fair thing to do to anyone so nice." Tonio looked down at the ground, shuffling his foot.

"Listen, if I didn't want your company, I'd tell you and go off on my own. I enjoy being with you. Besides, you're pretty handy to have around. Look at all the stuff I'll learn from you, like the Love Rock. I would never have known that if it wasn't for you." Her smile was so sweet and sincere that he believed her, and he felt a little more at ease. The last thing he wanted to do was drag anyone down into his abyss of darkness.

Tonio also liked being with her. It took his mind off the dull ache in his heart. Every morning it was all he could do to get up. He was actually excited about today when he first awoke. Today was definitely not yesterday. He had dulled his senses all day with Belini's and Tequila and sunned himself during the day on the beach. He enjoyed the numbness of not feeling like his heart had just been ripped out of his chest. No, today was not yesterday. Today was much better. He had enjoyed how Sidney's butt had looked in her shorts. He may be stricken with grief, but he was still a man who appreciated a woman who took care of herself and looked it.

"Thanks for being so understanding. I'll make it up to you somehow." Tonio slid her one of his side smiles.

Together they walked down to the cliffside and enjoyed the view. There wasn't a cloud in the sky, and the slight breeze that caressed their skin relaxed their thoughts and nourished their souls. Both were starting to succumb to the tranquility of this unique place. They stood there for quite some time taking it all in, in quiet reverence. In the background they heard their guide, Mike, calling the group to reassemble for their hike back. Before she could start off, she felt Tonio wrap his arm around her shoulder as he gave it a gentle squeeze. Looking down into her eyes, he said, "This trip would have had very little meaning for me if I didn't have you around to make me see all the beauty. Thank you." He leaned down toward her. She held her breath, stunned and not able to move a muscle at this unexpected physical contact. He pressed his lips gently to her forehead and then withdrew.

"I . . . I . . . you're welcome." was all Sidney could stammer out. What the devil was going on here? Was she missing the boat or something? She felt very hot and started to perspire. Stepping away from him, she took a deep breath and concentrated hard on the ocean in front of her. She heard her name being called. It seemed from far away. Lost in thought, she suddenly came to and looked straight into Tonio's eyes.

"I'm sorry if my actions were unwanted. You look upset. What can I do?" Tonio looked miserable.

"Look, just don't worry about it. It's just been a long time since I've been touched that way. I wasn't expecting it, and you caught me off guard. Please don't worry about it. It's not your fault that I have issues. I'm just used to my guard always being up, OK?" She forced a gentle laugh and was rewarded when he smiled back at her.

"OK, whatever you say. I won't touch you again unless you ask me to." They walked back to the assembled group and hiked back along the trail.

Once they returned to their hotel, Tonio excused himself, saying that he needed to be alone to think about things. Sidney said that she understood and went off to the restaurant to have a drink.

Theo came up to her and asked if he could sit with her while he was on his break, wanting to finish off the conversation that they had started the other night. She ordered a piña colada and indulged Theo in her world of advertisement back home. He told her that as a young boy, he'd always been interested in the field but had a sick mother and no father. So instead of continuing school, he had to work any way that he could to support his mother and two sisters.

"Wow. That must have been pretty hard," Sidney said after listening to Theo tell his story.

"Not really. You do what you have to do to keep going. I would have worked a hundred jobs to help my family. Besides, if I had continued on with my studies, I probably would've had a completely different life, and I wouldn't have met my wonderful wife and had my two handsome sons. So all in all, I'm extremely fortunate with how my life worked out. It just goes to show that your actions now truly make your life later. Your life *is* now."

Sidney felt touched by his insights and thoughtfully took another sip of her drink.

"Well, signora, it has been wonderful talking with you. Thank you for your time, but I must return to work now. Enjoy the rest of your day!" Theo said happily.

Sidney held up the rest of her drink and quickly swallowed her last sip to answer him. "Oh, you know I will. You have a wonderful day too. Cheers!"

Sidney relaxed a little until she remembered Tonio's parting comment, *I won't touch you again until you ask me too.* What the heck kind of statement was that? As if she was going to ask him to. He was a wounded man. To ask him to touch her and have it progress would be taking advantage of the situation ever so slightly. True, she was attracted to him, that she would admit. But her mind knew the boundaries, and her body for the most part had followed suit. She pondered his statement some more while gazing out into the ocean. After ten minutes went by, she decided that whatever happened happened. She wasn't going to waste any more time thinking about it. This was her vacation after all, and she was going to investigate the town tonight and hopefully do some shopping.

Sidney walked out of her hotel and started up the cobblestone road into the small town. The sun was still high enough in the sky to merit a couple more hours of daylight. The buildings in the town were usually one story but had tones of character. Catholic emblems were everywhere. She was a Deist herself, but she did believe in a higher being. She walked into a couple of shops and bought a couple of beautifully colored silk scarves for her aunt as well as for herself. There was also a miniature figure of the Love Rock that Tonio had pointed out to her earlier that day. It was well priced, and on a whim, she decided to purchase it for him and one for herself to always remember this time in her life. She was hoping he wouldn't take the gift the wrong way. She meant it partly as a joke and also to inspire him to believe that all was not lost and hopeless.

In one of the last shops she visited were maps of tours that were available to the tourists. She spied a boat cruise with dinner and dancing included. She picked up it up and a couple of other brochures that looked interesting to her.

On her way back, she stopped at a local tavern playing exciting music, and the people were having a wonderful time dancing. She was seated in a quieter area where she could look at the people and enjoy the darkened view while she sipped her wine. As she sat there, she remembered all the times where she had felt worn-out and tired in the last two years and thought how silly she had been not to take a break before this. In a way, it was kind of depressing. Not being one to focus on the negative, she enjoyed the rest of her wine and continued to walk the rest of the way back to her hotel.

FOREVER ITALY

5

The next morning she woke up late. She enjoyed her late slumber so much that it was hard for her to get up. Then she took the crisp clean air into her lungs and heard the gulls calling each other as they flew over the ocean. With a big long stretch, she pulled her relaxed body up from the bed. Next, she bathed and decided that today would be a great day for suntanning. She pulled out her pretty bikini that set her eyes off dramatically and grabbed her sunscreen, bottle of wine for refreshment, and the brochures from last night to go over while lying in the sun.

As she walked out onto the beach, she spied a familiar face. Then she saw his body. *Oh my lord in heaven!* Sidney thought to herself. She knew that he took care of his physique, but this was an understatement. He was all muscle, not an ounce of fat on him anywhere that she could see. She felt the prickles of desire course through her belly; her mouth had gone completely dry. A little shocked by the sudden rush of sensation, she tried to mask her feelings by smiling gently at him as she approached.

"Hey, stranger, you decided to enjoy the sunshine today too?" Tonio asked her smiling back. She couldn't see his eyes with his sunglasses on, which made her feel comfortable. She'd always had issues with men looking at her, especially now with so little clothing on.

"Do you mind if I join you?" Sidney looked at the ocean while it came up and met the sand.

"I don't mind at all." Tonio watched her as she laid her towel down. Her breasts nicely filled out her bikini top, and the rest of her was gorgeous as well. He felt himself becoming aroused and quickly, mentally gave his head a shake. He remembered what had happened yesterday and intended on keeping his word. He wouldn't touch her again unless she asked him to. At the moment though that was going to be tough for right then, she bent over to put sunscreen on her legs. Her cute little butt was aimed right in his line of sight. *Boy, oh boy,* he thought as he sucked in a long erotically charged breath.

Tonio cleared his throat and went back to the book he was reading. He knew that the longer he looked at her—well, let's just say that he might not be able to rein himself in.

Sidney lay down beside him on her back and reached into her bag for her sunglasses. She lay there and took some wonderfully deep breaths, taking in every sound and loving the caressing way the wind gently rushed at her skin. She felt her senses heighten and felt a sizzling current between them. She couldn't explain her feelings though barely a word had been spoken between them.

They lay like that for a little while. Tonio seemed to be enjoying his book, which was just fine with her as she was engrossed in her own tranquility. There were a handful of people on the beach; it was an intimate setting. This being a European country, some women preferred to go topless. Sidney wished that she had the courage to do it too. Maybe the wine would help her with that one. Thinking of the wine, she brought it out and uncorked it. Taking a healthy swallow, she offered some to Tonio. Surprised, he gladly accepted the drink, leaving his bottled water to stay cool in the sand beneath a corner of his towel. The sun was getting hotter, and she knew she'd better turn over and suntan her back. There was only one problem. She needed Tonio to apply the sunscreen.

"Tonio, could you please put sunscreen on my back? I can't reach it on my own."

Tonio passed the wine back and looked at her. "I have no problem with that as long as you don't."

She took a long guzzle of wine. To prove that she didn't, she passed him the sunscreen and turned over. He poured the liquid onto his palms, rubbing them together and then gently started with her shoulders. Then he was massaging it deeply into her skin, and she loved every minute of it. When she let a low moan escape from her lips, he instantly went hard and had to think of nonsexual things or ravage her body instead. He didn't think that she would be up for the latter, so he continued to rub her. Sidney reached behind to the strings of her bikini top and undid them, letting them fall to her sides. Tonio started to rub her back area and then down to her sides, grazing the edges of her breasts, sending heat down again into his loins. She could feel the circular motion of his fingertips against the sides of her breasts and felt her body respond like molten lava spreading down through her center.

He wished that he could be as unaffected as she seemed to be. But what Tonio didn't know was that she felt like a live wire. She had some experience with men, but nothing had felt like this, so intense and sexual. Sure, she had had sex with only a couple of men, but it had been more for their benefit than hers. Thinking that it would keep them around longer, she had given in to their pleas of self-gratification. She felt very naïve when it came to sex; her experience with them left much to be desired. A fact she wanted to rectify one day.

Tonio's hands were magic. She secretly longed to feel his hands on other places of her body, and lost in her secret world of desire, she just felt him feel her. Suddenly his hands weren't there any more, and she realized that he had finished. She wanted more; her body ached for more. She had the impression that he might be able to teach her some things, especially if he could make her turn into caramel drizzle just by applying her tanning lotion. She took another long drink of the wine and thought about it for a while.

The wine that she'd drunk quickly was starting to take an effect on her. Or it could have been the fact that she was so aroused that caused her to throw caution to the wind. Suddenly, without thought or care of her bikini top being undone, she turned right over onto her back, a smile of satisfaction on her face.

Tonio choked on his water. "I guess I need sunscreen on my breasts now too," Sidney said in a low voice. Tonio watched as she poured the lotion onto her hands and started to rub her breasts, making sure that she took the time to ensure that every surface was covered. When he saw her erect nipples responding to her own touch, it was almost his undoing. Sidney glanced at him and noticed his erection and asked him if he was all right.

"I think it might be time for me to go for a swim or take you up to my room and massage you under the rest of your bikini," Tonio said, looking straight at her as he got up and walked toward the ocean.

Holy cow, Sidney thought to herself. "Wait for me. I think I need to cool down too." Sidney got up naked except for her bottoms and caught up to Tonio.

They walked into the water together; both tried to keep a safe distance from each other. The water was clear and refreshing as it bathed their hot aroused bodies. Sidney felt like a carefree schoolgirl. They waded out into the tall waves, Sidney ahead of Tonio.

A large wave caught Sidney off balance and threw her right onto Tonio's chest. His arms came up automatically to encircle her naked flesh, her breasts resting against his. He could feel her nipples bud. Their eyes locked, their breathing became thick with lust. She couldn't help herself. She reached her arms around his neck and leaned into the best kiss she'd ever had in her life. Her lips gently sought his out. He pressed his own lips to hers. The kiss started out sweet and quickly turned into the raw heat that they felt for each other. His hands grasped her shoulders, her lower back; and then when he felt her tongue slip into his mouth, he moaned, grasping that delicious butt of hers and pressed her against him. Sidney could feel his hardness and felt her control slipping as she started to move her hips against him. Their tongues were doing their magical dance; the cool water seemed to simmer with the heat radiating from their bodies. Tonio moved one hand from her butt and brought it up to caress one of her breasts. Sidney, in her bold state, moved her hands all over his back and down to cup his erection. Tonio gasped. It shocked him so much that he pulled his head back as he let out a guttural moan. Sidney took the opportunity to kiss his neck and collarbone. She stroked his manhood, surprised by the strength of it. He cupped this hand with his own and looked down into her heat-laden eyes. "We have to stop before we can't," Tonio said, gasping for breath. Sidney gave him one last gentle squeeze and then wrapped both arms around him, resting her body against his. Her head lay against his chest. They breathed together as one, labored and raspy as the ocean slowly helped to cool the turmoil in their beings.

Tonio brought his hands up to cup her head and slowly, gently, moved her back so that he could look into her smiling eyes. "That was something else. I don't know what came over us, but I know that I would like to continue this at some point. It doesn't even feel weird to me that we haven't known each other that long. I just feel so comfortable with you," Tonio whispered softly.

Sidney pulled back gently. "I know how you feel. And don't worry, I know that a relationship between the two of us is not something that you're ready to do at the moment. How would you feel about just letting things go where they may? I have to warn you though. I may need some help in the sexual department."

"How do you mean, are you a virgin?" Tonio questioned with great interest.

"No, but practice makes perfect right?" Sidney's smile was shy and inviting.

"We've only got two days left together. I guess we'll see, won't we?"

"You never can tell. Let's just enjoy our time and not worry about the future right now. No games, no expectations. Just you and me and this . . ." She gestured to her half-naked body. "Are you interested?"

Tonio was a little bit shocked by her candidness. He tried to cover it by faking a cough. Her proposal was sound, and it was every man's dream. This made sense to Tonio. It was a no-strings-attached attraction, probably just what he needed to help him forget his previous life. He really liked her and had never believed in love at first sight and had no intention of starting anything for a long time to come. But this, he could do this. "I like the way you think. Count me in."

Tonio and Sidney played in the water for a while. They embraced several times, feeling free to do to each other whatever came naturally. It was a perfect day, and they both felt perfectly happy. There was a sense of freedom in their situation that they both reveled in.

When they got back to the beach, Sidney and Tonio went over the brochures that she had picked up the previous night. They decided to go on the dinner/dance boat cruise on their last night, thinking that that would be the perfect send-off from one another. Today though, they just simply wanted to enjoy each other's company and got dressed for dinner in town.

Sidney loved the cozy seaside place they'd decided on for dinner. It was rustic and classy all at the same time. Buoys hung from the ceiling, candles and fresh flowers sat on each table. Their table was situated outside where lights hung from the nearby trees and gave it a romantic setting.

Sidney looked at the wine menu and again spied the Cortina d'Ampezzo wine that she loved so much. "Tonio, did you receive this wine in your room too? I just think it's fantastic," Sidney asked with enthusiasm.

"Yes. I have tried some. It's very full-bodied and has a great reputation here in Italy. It's locally made by a family here and has branched out all across Europe. It's done very well. I'd sure like to have stock in that company. I'd be a millionaire." Tonio laughed.

"Tell me a little more about you, Sidney. I feel like all we've done is talk about me and my horrible life. How do you see life working out for you?" Tonio queried.

"Well, to tell you the truth, I haven't had a lot of time to give it a substantial amount of thought. I believe that I want what most women want at my stage of the game. I've had the freedom of having pursued a great career, financial security, and a great family. My aunt's getting married soon, and I love the fact that I get an instant family with her kids. Life's going pretty good so far." Sidney looked content with this answer and took a sip of her wine.

"That's great and all, but what about the man situation? Don't you want someone to spend your life with?" Tonio couldn't believe that she hadn't mentioned this as a part of her future. They both knew what they were doing was fun and would have no lasting impact past thirty-six hours. At least that's what he thought she wanted. Wasn't it? Tonio gave her a long look, waiting for her to respond.

"It just hasn't been in the cards for me so far. Oh, sure I've had a couple of relationships, but my work always got in the way, and I never had time for them. They would always get bored and leave for the next best thing. I really didn't blame them. Why would anyone want to be with someone who never was around, let alone be in the same state? So if it happens, it happens. It's certainly not because I don't want a relationship. I just need to find someone who really loves me enough to stay around when the going gets tough. Hopefully, one day I'll find the right mix and not run away myself," Sidney explained.

"What exactly do you mean? Did you have a bad experience?" Tonio looked at her with concern in his eyes.

Sidney suddenly looked very young and sad. "When I was a kid, my parents went on a skiing trip and were killed in an avalanche. Life never was the same again. As soon as anyone gets too close to me romantically, I usually run myself in the other direction. I'm afraid that the ones I love will be taken away. Scared to trust, scared to love. It's not the greatest combination, that's for sure, but it's who I am." Sidney took a long drink of her wine, finished it off, and motioned to the waiter for another glass.

Tonio saw her pain. He reached across the table and gently took her hand in his own and slowly rubbed his thumb against her soft skin. "I'm so sorry for your loss ... in all aspects," Tonio said, giving his condolences. "I've got those feelings running through me now too after what I've just been through with Angelica. I feel so angry even saying her name. I too have felt the loss of a parent, my dad. It all happened a couple of years ago in a hot tub. They, my mom and dad, were on a skiing vacation as well. My dad loved hot tubs. One night, he stayed in a little too long and had a heart attack. My mother had gotten out earlier, going to the washroom. By the time she got back, it was too late. My mom always blames herself. If only she'd been there, she might have been able to save him. We'll never know now at any rate. I loved him so much and always will." Tonio choked on his own emotions with his last strained statement. Their hands were still together, and she squeezed his hand gently with what she hoped was reassuring support.

"It sucks, doesn't it?" Sidney said with conviction.

"You can say that again," Tonio agreed.

Sidney repeated the statement again, and they both laughed.

They talked more about Sidney's aunt and new instant family and his family too. Sidney learned that he came from a small family as well. He had one brother named Mike who was an airline pilot. His father had been a teacher, and his mother had stayed at home to take care of the family. His brother flew for American Air and had many routes all over the place. He was married, with three children, and lived in New York, New York.

Now that his father had passed away, Tonio stayed in the same city to be near his mom, though his brother often commented on how much he'd like them all to be together. But Tonio's mother, Verucha, had a full life where they were and wanted to stay, at least for a while. So Tonio and his mother stayed in Athens, Greece, and enjoyed their lives. Tonio had talked to his mother a few times since his disastrous wedding fiasco. She had sounded just as broken up as Tonio was. She only wanted her children to be happy, and she thought that she might finally have some grandchildren nearby. Now she advised him to carry on with his life for things usually got better with time.

Sidney and Tonio ordered their dinner and after shared a delicious pastry for dessert.

After dinner, they walked along the shore back to their hotel, arm in arm. They had talked of too many painful things and took comfort in each other's understanding. That was enough. They talked some more into a star-laden night at their hotel restaurant, sipping piña coladas and snacking on nachos. They then bid each other goodnight and promised to meet the next morning for breakfast.

After eating the next morning, they rented a car for the day to see more sights of Italy.

Tonio, of course, was the designated tour guide—a fact that he didn't mind. He liked teaching people just like his father had. By the end of their day, they were exhausted. They visited a couple of churches, museums, and of course, bakeries. Sidney loved the scones and Italian ice cream as did Tonio. As they drove through the small towns, they enjoyed a similar sense of humor. You know the feeling of when someone "gets you." Well, that is exactly what Sidney and Tonio felt toward one another. Tonio had a way of making everything interesting, and he sure could make her laugh. Like at the museum for example, they had played a game of who-was-it? Tonio had fibbed righteously a couple of times, and Sidney eventually caught on to his charade. She laughed at him and his silliness. They were becoming fast friends, which was great because the attraction that they felt for one another was stronger than ever. So much so that Sidney was having a hard time digesting the fact that in forty-eight hours, they would be off on their own adventures—alone. Oh, she knew that Tonio was definitely not ready for a relationship. That was obvious. But there was a part of her that kind of wished the circumstances were a lot different. So she made herself think only of the precious time that remained and enjoyed herself completely.

The next day, they sun tanned, just relaxing and relishing in each other's company. She felt connected to Tonio. He was a very sweet and caring man. Yesterday, he had picked up stray bits of ice cream on his finger and had eaten it Watching him suck his own finger made Sidney weak in the knees. She remembered what those lips and fingers could do all too well. They'd shared really tender and memorable moments.

She had felt special and cared for. It was nice to have someone's full attention, even if it was for a short time. She hoped he was having a wonderful time too.

"Do you need more lotion on your back? You're looking a little pink."

"Yes, please," Sidney replied, touched at his thoughtfulness.

Tonio applied the sunscreen, giving her a gentle rubdown. He really liked her. Too bad for all the turmoil that had recently happened in his life; they might have had a real chance. He wasn't one for jumping into relationships simply for the purpose of trying to forget and mask the pain of the previous one. He was mature enough to realize when the heart and soul truly needed a break. Besides, he wasn't into getting hurt again any time soon. Relationships were trouble with a capital *T*. Still, he had a feeling that he would always wonder what might have been with Sidney.

"I'm going to miss you, you know?" Sidney mumbled against her towel.

"You mean my massages or my tour guiding skills?" Tonio questioned back.

"You know what I mean. We get along so well. That's usually the hard part in relationships. We like a lot of the same things, and we're both hardworking people. That's important to me. I like it when the people I associate with have just as much going on as I do. Plus, don't blush, you're very sweet and considerate."

Tonio leaned down and gave her a lingering kiss on the cheek. He felt warm inside from her comments and was touched.

"Why thank you, I'm pretty sweet on you too. It's going to be lonely without you in Venice. Maybe we could e-mail each other once in a while to stay in contact?"

"That would be fine with me." Sidney felt a wave of sadness wash over her. Damn that Angelica for what she had done to this man.

"Where are you off to next?" Tonio asked.

"Well, there's a couple of wineries that I want to take a tour of down in Tuscany."

"Sounds like a good time. It's right up your alley."

Sidney sighed and pressed her lips. If only they could have had more time together and under different circumstances. She knew that Tonio would find love again; he was too good-natured and fun not to. She really enjoyed how relaxed she felt when she was in his presence, and he seemed to feel the same way.

They lazed away the rest of the day and had a late dinner in town. Then they walked for hours and talked about all sorts of topics from politics to religion.

They parted company late into the night. Sidney and Tonio both had shopping to do in various parts of the town the next day and were meeting again later in the afternoon for their dinner and sleepover cruise.

When Sidney was in town walking down the shop-lined street, she saw the most beautiful green dress. It was light and breezy and the type of dress that one couldn't wear a bra with. It made her feel sexual and lighthearted. She wanted this night to be special, one that Tonio wouldn't forget for a long time to come no matter who came into his life. Her heart hurt at the thought of not seeing Tonio again. Life just didn't seem fair. Just when she found someone special, she had to let him go. He wasn't available. He was wounded within his soul. No, it could not, would not work out. Someone was going to end up hurt, and she had no interest in that. As she processed her thoughts, she secretly admitted to herself that she had never intended on getting this emotionally attached to him. It was just one of those things that she hadn't expected, and it was all that more precious because of it.

She was still trying to keep him emotionally at arms length, even now. She honestly didn't want to be involved in anything this complicated. Even so, she found herself delving deeper and deeper into the unknown. She had to shake her head a couple of times. What did she think was going to happen? Move to Greece and bear his children? No, she didn't think so, even if it was a nice thought. She was getting carried away with her thoughts, and she knew it.

She and Tonio had booked the cruise when things were just starting to heat up between them and had only booked one room for the two of them to share. The very thought of sharing a bed with Tonio made her excited and nervous at the same time. The air was definitely sexually charged whenever they were around each other lately. Knowing that they were most likely to make love to one another tonight, Sidney was glad that she was on the pill. It was especially handy in situations such as this.

Looking at her watch, she discovered that it was fast approaching two, and she started to head back to get ready for the evening.

6

Tonio met Sidney in the hotel lobby. When she came down the stairs in her new dress, the air seemed to disappear in his lungs, and his heart did a hiccup. *Boy, was he in trouble*, he thought to himself. The green of her dress made her hair look like it was on fire; he longed to reach out and touch its wildness. This lady was a free bird, and he loved being around her. But he couldn't love her, could he? Absolutely not! It was far too soon. Hell, he would have been married a week and on his honeymoon in this exact spot with Angelica at this exact moment if things had gone through for heaven's sake. He knew that his emotions were completely unstable, which was why he was letting it happen at all. Sure they cared for one another in a completely no-attachments way. It was perfect. No one would get hurt, would they?

Tonio couldn't handle these thoughts at the moment and brought his mind back to reality. Sidney was breathtaking, and he leaned down to quickly kiss her. Instead, the kiss turned into a melt-your-knees, pass-out kind of kiss as Sidney wrapped her arms around his neck. She too was drawn into the natural chemistry that swept them both away on a current of unrelenting lust.

As they drew away from each other, Sidney's green eyes took on a whole other color of jade. Her feelings of lust were exposed for all to see, especially Tonio. He cleared his throat. "I think it's time we were on our way, don't you?"

"Yes. You're absolutely right." Feeling more than a little stirred up, Sidney leaned down to grab her bag that had fallen onto the ground during their onslaught of each other.

They enjoyed the journey through the small towns as the bus wound its way along the coastline to their launch destination. They chatted comfortably with one another. They both agreed that one day they would each love to have a small piece of this country for themselves. The ease at which they conversed with one another didn't escape either of them. They were usually laughing with one another, shared and challenged each other's views, and really were becoming the best of friends. The fact that this was their last night together made them each relish the precious moments that were left.

The bus pulled up at a stop along the road for its passengers to disembark. Sidney couldn't take her eyes away from their boat, which was in fact a huge yacht. It was gorgeous. She and Tonio walked down the dusty path and onto the boarding dock. There were about six other couples with them though neither one of them really noticed. They were completely involved with each other's company and only politely smiled at the others when laughing at something the other had said.

One of the deckhands showed them to their room for the night. The yacht had two levels. The top deck held the accommodations for crew and passengers alike. Their room was dressed in beautiful Italian fabrics and comfortable furniture, with a single king-size bed in the middle of the room. Their room had oversized windows, which meant they had great views by day and night.

They unpacked the necessary toiletries out of their suitcases. Sydney and Tonio felt quite fortunate to have their last night together in such picture-perfect surroundings.

It was near lunchtime, and they were both starving as they headed down to the lower deck. All the couples had their own tables to dine at which they were both grateful for. They wanted to spend the last bits of their time together engrossed with each other only and didn't want to make idle chitchat with strangers. Sidney pored over the wine list, checking to see if they had the lovely label that she had grown so fond of. Of course, they did; and she heartily ordered a whole bottle of it, not just a glass.

"Boy, someone's sure going to drink me under the table tonight. Whatever happened to pacing yourself?" Tonio questioned with a knowing grin.

"Well, I guess that means that you'll just have to keep up with me," Sidney said, flipping her hair off her shoulder. Here eyes were dancing with mischief, daring him to accept her challenge.

He loved that about her. She really seemed to enjoy life, especially the alcohol parts. Not that she was a heavy drinker, only that she knew what she liked. And Tonio loved that quality.

They ate lunch of escargot, clams, and pena pasta in tomato sauce. Everything was delicious and left them both sated. They felt they were busting at the seams and felt the need to walk around the gorgeous vessel. It was painted with blue, white, and green waves on the side, beautiful wood adorned the edging and handrails. The wood was so lacquered that it shined in the sun and felt smooth to the touch. The ship was lovingly cared for, and it showed. Tonio really liked boats and wanted to have his one day.

He held her in his arms next to the rail, and even though the breeze was cool, he could still feel the heat radiating off her skin.

The rest of the day went by, and it was a sightseeing extravaganza. They hit port for restocking and then were quickly on their way again with nothing but open sea ahead. Tonio and Sidney decided to skip dinner as they were still full from their lunch, but both planned to return to dance the night away. Sidney put on one of her special purchases, a number that was sure to impress Tonio. It was backless with a deep V that hugged her bosom; its creamy color set off her new tan. They danced mostly to upbeat songs, trying to keep the mood between them light. Then, a ballad with its rich tones lulling them dreamily around the dance floor and into each other's arms. Tonio was so strong; in his arms she felt safe and happy. She let herself drift off on a sigh and relaxed into his embrace, resting her head on his shoulder.

Tonio felt her release. Mentally and physically sensing her surrender, he couldn't help himself. He gently stroked the length of her spine, and as she brought her head up, he let his full lips find her own and gave into his desires. She didn't protest or try to draw away, merely succumbed to the fire inside. The kiss was gentle yet held promises both could never ignore. The kiss seemed to last forever. His lips, soft and probing, sought out her own warmth; their tongues flickered against one another. A small moan escaped her throat, and they both realized that the song had ended. Gazing back into one another's eyes, she spied the silent question in his. She smiled up at him and grasped his hand in hers, leading him off the dance floor and up to their room.

As soon as the door closed behind them, they were engulfed in each other's embrace. Hands were roving over clothing that silently and quickly slipped to the floor, her dress a pile at their feet. He held her back from him and let his gaze skim over her naked flesh; his appreciation of her beauty, obvious. The thin cloth of his underwear couldn't hide his large erection. She cupped it, and Tonio moaned his approval. She was just about to take it off when he collected her into his arms and walked over to the bed. He gently layed her down and looked into her eyes as he took off this last garment of clothing. He layed down on top of her, their lips joining in a smoldering kiss as his head gently, rhythmically brushed her innermost being. He grasped her ripe breasts and took turns sucking her pointed peaks. She grasped his butt and strained to control her breathing. She was so overcome she thought that she would faint. His fingers slipped lower and played their own magical tune as he made her ready for him. Pure ecstasy throbbed in their veins, both wanting and seeking more. Tonio continued his onslaught. Suddenly she saw dots of light behind her closed eyes as she reached an earth-shattering climax. Tonio stroked her hair, waiting for her to come back to earth. He was poised and ready to enter her. He looked straight into her eyes and gently cradled her beautiful face in his hands.

"Sidney, what do you want?" Tonio asked, his voice breathlessly strained.

"I want you and nothing else."

With that, Tonio gently slid into to her, slowly, ever so slowly; he didn't want to rush or hurt her. Together they formed their own rhythm until the sheets were amassed around them; their passion and heat knew no bounds. They clung to one another as if their lives depended upon it. They both reached the end of their journey together and collapsed upon one another, their chests heaving and their skin damp with passionate sweat. They lay together without saying anything for a while. Both knowing that there wasn't much to say, they both knew the score.

No, there were no attachments or strings here, only pure raw passionate sex with someone they both felt comfortable with. They made love two more times before the sun came up. Finally satiated, they fell asleep, the kind of sleep that is completely content.

The next morning she felt Tonio sliding his fingers around her breasts, down her tummy, and onto the nether regions of her body. She felt herself begin to melt again. Knowing that this was a precursor to many pleasurable things, she lay there and finally responded back when she couldn't take any more. This time though, she climbed on top of his being and was so tantalizing in her mannerisms that Tonio almost lost himself several times. She wanted to please him as much as he had her. She licked his nipples and gyrated her hips. He clasped her butt in an attempt to take control of the situation, but in the end, the feeling was so exquisite that he ended up flowing with her and letting her take him to the heights of heaven and back again. Then he floated back to sleep.

Tonio awoke to wet droplets on his arm. Curious, he looked down at Sidney and realized they were her tears.

"I'm sorry, Tonio, I just can't seem to help myself. My heart is hurting so much I feel it's going to burst out of my chest. Just ignore me please, I'm being silly. I knew going in what we were doing. I just can't imagine that I won't see you again." Sidney tried to brush the tears away. Realizing that it wasn't going to work, on a muffled moan, she sprang from the bed and into the bathroom to drown her sorrows in the blast of the hot shower.

Tonio watched her go. He too was feeling pained. He got up from the bed and walked into the bathroom. Sidney didn't hear him come in and was surprised when she felt his arms close around her. She turned in his embrace and hung onto him while she felt the release of her tears flow down his chest and down the drain. When eventually she looked up, she saw to her amazement that he too had tears in his eyes that threatened to overspill.

"Oh, Tonio. We are such fools. What have we done to ourselves?" They hung onto one another until both had quieted their souls. They were, in fact, completely miserable. Sidney felt she'd fallen the hardest. Tonio was used to heartache. That's all he had felt for the last two weeks except for maybe a moment or two of happiness with her.

Tonio and Sidney held hands the whole way back on the bus to the hotel. They were seated in silence, both lost in their own thoughts.

Tonio was hurting a lot more than he let on. He didn't want to make things harder than they already had to be. His heart couldn't take any more. He just wanted to get away, away from this women that made sense being in his life. He wanted to be with her always. He even felt, although it rationally seemed impossible, that he had fallen in love with Sidney. They were so close. Yes, he truly felt deep emotions for her. He knew though that if he told her these things, she wouldn't believe him. Talk about bad timing. Damn Angelica. It seemed that she had led him here to Sidney only for her to be taken away from him due to the absurdity of the situation. Sidney couldn't possibly take him seriously. Maybe in another place in time they could be together, but it definitely wasn't now.

Before either one of them knew it, they were back at the hotel. It was time to say goodbye. Tonio had already packed his things and taken them on the cruz with him, he didn't need much. His flight was leaving in two hours and he had to get to the airport now. The timing was perfect, it would make saying goodbye a lot easier, or so he thought.

Through a veil of tears, Sidney whispered, "I don't know when or how, but I know that one day you will be happy again. I want you to know that this has been one of the best times of my entire life. If you ever need me, you know where I am." On a broken sob, she fell into Tonio's arms.

"My sweet love, if only we were in different circumstances." Tonio cradled her head to his chest. "You will always have a special place in my heart." Tonio held back his tears.

"Tonio, I almost forgot." Sidney reached into her purse for the box that she had wrapped herself. "Here. You can remember me through this. Don't open it now. Wait until you're on the plane. It'll be easier that way."

He leaned down and gave her one last lingering kiss. A kiss that he hoped conveyed all that his heart was screaming at him to say. But he could not. It was not the right time; it would never be. She would just think that he was a fool, and how could you love a fool?

He walked away from her then. He looked back at her for just a second, a glance to remember her by. What he saw broke his heart, and he vowed that one day he would see her again when they were both happy.

FOREVER ITALY

7

Sidney spent the last two days at the hotel going back to the places that they had visited and eaten at together. She just couldn't bring herself to let him go just yet. She held back her feelings for him as the timing just sucked. She knew she'd played with fire and unfortunately definitely had been burned. He was healing from a failed altar attempt, how could the right time be now? She knew it all was just crazy. Maybe she'd just relished in the challenge of it all. No, she knew this wasn't the case. She had enjoyed his company so much it was just natural that love had snuck up on her. In life, timing is everything; and because of it, she couldn't have any of it. She was beginning to wonder what happened to the part of her that ran away when things got too complicated. Normally she was the one running in the other direction. Now here she was pinning after someone that was totally unavailable to her in all meanings of the words.

She walked up and down the beaches, reminiscing and trying to understand her feelings for this wonderful man. She thought of all the fun and laughter that they had shared together; in a way, he had saved her. He was her hero. She had proven to herself that she could stick when the going got tough, even if she couldn't tell him her true feelings. For telling Tonio would only put off the necessary healing that needed to happen for him to be whole again. If he had just conveyed any form of love to her, she knew that it would have opened the floodgates of her heart and that she would have told him of her love for him as well.

But in their strength of love, it had equated to silence. Space and time were needed now. These would set them free, allowing time to heal, and maybe one day see each other once again. Oh, she knew it wouldn't be any time soon, but that's what hope was all about, and she had plenty of that because of him. In a short span of time, he had forever changed her. She was no longer afraid of love. For she saw the power of it and what it could do to heal one another by setting each other free.

She smiled through her tears and thought of the Love Rock. He truly did carry her heart with him, and she hoped that maybe for even a single moment of time, he had felt the same way.

Sidney packed her cases and said her goodbyes. She had made many friends here during her short two-week stay. But life carried on and so must she. She called for a cab and was soon heading toward her new destination, alone. Her heart felt heavy, and she wished for the happiness that she had felt with Tonio.

An hour and a half later, she had arrived at the largest winery in Italy—at least that's what the brochure said. It was huge, waving hill after waving hill, just covered in vines. It was a gorgeous sight to behold. She knew that it probably took a lot of manpower to run this establishment. And then above it all was the beautiful mountain that loomed overhead. It almost seemed as if the mountain was protecting the valley below. It looked monstrous and mysterious all at the same time.

Sidney paid the cabdriver and walked into the foyer of what she guessed was the main house. It was very Italian in its décor, very soft yet colorful with undercurrents of strength and nobility.

Sidney was greeted by a middle-aged lady who had the same glint in her eyes as signora Chiara.

"My name is Mary, signora. Please feel free to stay as long as you would like. I know you have other day trips planned for the surrounding wineries, but I assure you, you will find nothing as beautiful as this," Mary informed her while busying herself with hotel keys and linens.

She showed Sidney to her room, which was magnificent. It was made up of different shades of white and blues that had a very relaxing effect. Mary went to the french doors and opened them wide. Sidney couldn't believe what she saw. There before her was her own little piece of nirvana. It had a gorgeous pool, lawn chairs, air mattresses, and all sorts of aids to help one relax.

"I can't believe all this. I know where I'll be spending a lot of my time! Now this is a vacation." Plus she knew that it would help ease her heart to be surrounded by luxury, or so she thought.

Just then, three ladies around Sidney's age came out to greet her. They had been out in the kitchen and had heard of her arrival. "Sidney Hamilton, it's a pleasure to meet you." She stuck out her hand in greeting and shook the three girls' hands. She noticed something very familiar about them but couldn't place her finger on it.

Rosa, the eldest, led the conversation. "The pleasure is all ours. If you're up for a tour tomorrow, we would be glad to show you around. Plus we can do some wine tasting," she said with a devilish glint in her eyes. Sidney was suspicious of her right away.

"I'll let you know, thanks for the offer. Right now, all I want to do is relax. Nice to meet you Rosa, Anna, and Mia. I'm sure I'll be seeing you soon." And with that, Sidney walked back into her suite.

She started unpacking and went to her dresser. On top of it, she saw the same wine that she had drunk most of her trip. It said on the note beside it, "Cortina d'Ampezzo on the house." Suddenly it hit Sidney that this was the winery that made it. After all this time, she'd never clued in being so lost in her own thoughts. *Well, why waste it*, she thought to herself. She opened to bottle and put on her bikini. Next, she pulled back the shears to make sure that she had the pool area to herself. There weren't a lot of guests here at this time; most of them had already headed out, and a new batch would be arriving in a few days. This suited Sidney just fine. She needed time to think anyway, to be alone with her thoughts.

She grabbed her beach towel and sunscreen and headed out to a lounger to relax. She didn't bother with a glass; she and the bottle of wine had a date on the lounger. As she lay there getting hotter by the minute, suddenly she remembered her sunscreen and then she wondered, *Who would apply it? Oh well, you can't win them all*. She applied it as best she could and then lay back to enjoy the rays of the sun warming her skin.

After a while, she was getting hot. The blue coolness of the water beckoned to her. She felt only slightly tipsy having only drunk half the bottle of wine, so she didn't even consider not going in for a dip. She dived into the water. Its coldness was a welcome shock on her burning skin.

What she didn't realize was that the pool wasn't deep enough for straight down diving. It was only four feet deep. Sidney felt the cement against her skull, and then there was nothing at all. She passed out cold under the water.

* * *

Aunt Thelma and Maurice were starting to get very worried about Sidney. They hadn't heard from her in a week and a half week. Aunt Thelma was pacing the kitchen as she prepared their dinner. "It's just not like her to not call when she said she would. I just know that something has happened. My gut instincts are going into overdrive. What could be so important that she doesn't have five minutes to call us?" She was completely frustrated, almost to the point of tears.

"Maybe if we just give it a couple more days, give her some more time. If we haven't heard anything by Wednesday, then we'll get on the phone to the hotels that she was supposed to be staying in." Maurice tried to sooth her, but he knew it was no use; she had been a nervous wreck since yesterday.

"I promised myself that when we came together that I would never let anything bad happen to her. She's lost so much already." Aunt Thelma let loose a few of the tears she'd been holding back. She felt Maurice's arms embrace her, and she turned into his comforting sanctuary and let out the restof her tears.

She dried her eyes with the Kleenex that he handed her. Somewhere off in the distance, they heard the phone ringing; both of them looked at each other, hoping that maybe the fates had heard their plea. Aunt Thelma raced to the phone before the answering machine could pick up. At first she thought no one was there. She heard muffled noises in the background, and then someone unfamiliar spoke.

"Is this Sidney Hamilton's Aunt Thelma?" the voice questioned.

"Yes, it is. Who am I speaking to?" Thelma couldn't keep the panic out of her voice.

"Your niece has been in an accident, signora. She dove into a pool that wasn't deep enough and unfortunately has lapsed into a coma. She is at Le Costa Hospital here in Italy. We wish for you to come immediately."

Thelma started shaking and dropped the phone. Maurice saw her collapse to the ground with heart-shattering sobs. He raced to her and picked up the phone to hear for himself what had happened to his new niece. After obtaining all the details, he took Thelma to the bedroom and insisted that she stay put on the bed while he made the necessary arrangements with the airlines and the hair salon. He dragged out the suitcases and asked her to help him pack for a long stay in Italy. What the outcome would be, both could only imagine.

They arrived in Italy a day and a half later, both had barely slept. The stress of the unknown ate away at them. From the airport, they caught a cab to the hospital. Once inside, they got directions to their niece's nursing station.

"You must be Mr. and Mrs. Coleman. I'm Francesca, Sidney's nurse for the day. I'm so glad that you could make it." Franchesca shook their hands and motioned for them to follow her.

"How is she?" Thelma asked breathlessly.

"She's still in a coma, has been for the last week. Eros, the man who found her, saved her life. He came to say hello. Apparently, they met on the plane to Italy. His family owns the vineyard where she had just arrived at. Anyway, he saw her motionless at the bottom of the pool and dove in. Once he got her out, he did CPR and brought her back. No one knows for sure how long she was in the pool. They did a lot of blood work as you can imagine, and they found alcohol in her system. We don't think she did this intentionally, but we do have to ask you a lot of uncomfortable questions. Why don't we go in the family lounge and talk?"

After Thelma had talked with the nurse and assured her that her niece was not an alcoholic or suicidal, they were escorted to see Sidney for the first time. They heard the machines first beeping away, notifying all that she was still alive. Thelma and Maurice were shocked by what they saw. Her head was bandaged with tubes and wires coming out from all sorts of places on her body. Her eyes were bruised and swollen. She was hooked up to a ventilator to support her breathing; a drainage tube had been placed into her skull to relieve any mounting pressure, and a catheter had also been inserted to help her "go to the bathroom." She also had IV fluids, but it was still necessary to insert a nasogastric tube down her nose to allow her to eat. Three probes had been placed on her chest and stomach to monitor breathing, heart rate, and blood oxygen levels. She was, in short, a mess.

"Oh my god." It was all Thelma could get out. She sat in the nearest chair to her niece's bedside and grasped her hand. Maurice came up to stand behind Thelma and placed his hands on her shoulders, trying to steady her.

"The doctors had to perform emergency surgery. When she came in, her pulse was quite weak, and we did an MRI to confirm the swelling on her brain. That's why you see the tube there in her skull. We don't know how much damage has been done. She could have all sorts of problems from being paralyzed to mentally disabled, or she could walk out of here in one piece. No one knows for sure. We honestly don't even know if she'll ever wake up. There might be some hard decisions ahead. The truth is we just don't know. We're very sorry." Franchesca grasped Thelma's hand and gave it a reassuring squeeze. "What we do believe, however, is that she can hear, even recognize familiar voices. Studies show that people in a coma remember voices when they wake up. The conversations aren't always coherent, but they knew that a loved one was nearby and next to them. I have to attend to her now so just pretend that I'm not here." Francesca busied herself with her duties.

"How could this happen to her, Maurice? She was on vacation for Christ's sake." Trying to keep her anger and frustration at bay, she occupied herself with straightening Sidney's blankets. The room she was in was bland, so she made a mental note to bring in some flowers and put some pictures on the wall to brighten things up.

"It's me, Sidney, your Aunt Thelma. I could think of better ways for you to get me to come and see you in Italy." Aunt Thelma tried to keep her voice light, for if Sidney could in fact hear her, then she wanted the conversation to be of a light loving nature. "I hope you can hear me in there."

Both Maurice and Thelma kept a constant vigil by her bedside, only retiring to their nearby hotel at night for a restless sleep. They talked to her about anything and everything that they could. Hoping that one day, she would open those beautiful green eyes. Thelma decorated her room in the bright designer colors that she used to love and use in her advertising campaigns, anything that might be familiar to her. She even used baby powder to cleanse her hair; it was the next best thing to shampoo when you couldn't use the real thing.

Days turned into weeks, weeks turned into months, and Thelma and Maurice did have to make some hard choices. They were running out of money. It was either stay in Italy and be poor or go back to the States and be without

Sidney, leaving her behind. It really wasn't a hard decision to make. They sold the hair salon and their apartment. With the money they made from the sale of both, they were able to buy a beautiful house overlooking the ocean. Both would have been thrilled if only the circumstances had been different.

They had fallen into a routine of visiting during the day; then, they would come home for dinner and then head back again for a couple more hours in the evening. It was during one of the dinnertimes that she received an e-mail for Sidney from her work. They were very sad to hear of Sidney's condition and were still holding her job for her in the eventuality that she would hopefully return.

They were going through Sidney's e-mail files and wanted to send out an e-mail to her close friends that she had mentioned in past conversations. Thelma scrolled down and noticed that there were a few from a man named Tonio. She wondered if he was someone that her niece had met on her travels. She e-mailed him the following letter:

Dear Mr. Tonio:

My curiosity has gotten the better of me, which is why I'm e-mailing you. You are obviously a friend of my niece, so it is with regret that I am informing you of her near-fatal accident. She dove into a pool that wasn't deep enough, and she hit her head on the cement bottom. To say the least, she is pretty banged up and has been in a coma for the last two months in La Costa Hospital here in Italy.

My husband and I have now moved here to be close to her. There is still hope that she will awaken, but no one is sure of the damage that she might have sustained. She is still on life support and is feeding through a tube in her nose. She is so young and has most of her life ahead of her. We are all hoping for a positive outcome.

Hope to hear back from you soon. Sorry to inform you this way.

Thelma and Maurice Coleman

Tonio finished reading the e-mail and sat in shock, staring at the computer screen. Ten minutes went by, and he felt something hitting his pants. He realized they were his tears. His beautiful Sidney, what in the hell had happened? Oh, he knew what the screen said, its cold, uncaring black-and-white letters jumped off the screen almost mockingly. If only he hadn't left her, this wouldn't have happened; he hadn't wanted to. Now he knew how his mom had felt when his father had passed away in the hot tub. Useless.

He quickly called his editor and travel agency to explain the situation and was booked on the next flight out.

He had to go to her. There was no doubt in his mind that it was the right thing to do. Besides, he blamed himself for this happening to her at all. He hadn't fully realized until now how protective he was of her. Her light had somehow seeped into his soul, making him feel things that he shouldn't for her. He just knew that she needed him. Maybe she would wake up before he got there.

In the two months that had passed, he'd uncovered more unsightly truths about Angelica. She wasn't the person he thought she was. He wished that he'd never met her in the first place, but then he wouldn't have met Sidney. For that, he was totally grateful to her!

Angelica had been having an affair for a few months. She'd said that it wasn't anything that Tonio had done. Only that she wasn't ready to settle down at the moment. Tonio tried his best to understand her feelings, but cheating was just something that he could never do himself. In the end, she had done him a favor by coming clean on their wedding day. It had opened the door to meet Sidney. He wished Angelica the best of what she deserved.

As for himself, he considered himself healed. He took a page from Sidney's book and decided to apply it to his own life, by just getting on with it. He'd been alone writing one night with a bottle of wine and a fine cigar glowing in the ashtray. All the anger and resentment he'd felt for Angelica flowed onto the pages and out of his heart for good. Since hearing of Angelica's indecencies, he'd quickly decided not to waste any more time on her. He took a lot of long walks and decided that he didn't need to try to find himself. He already knew who he was and liked what he saw in the mirror in the morning. The rest of the world be damned!

Right now, Sidney was all he could think about. He knew the e-mail was a sign to be with her. She had helped him on her own vacation for heaven's sake! He'd be on the plane in less than twelve hours, and he was starting to get impatient.

* * *

Back at Le Costa Hospital, Sidney still hadn't come out of her coma. The doctors had just recently ordered more blood work to see what her white and red blood cell counts were. Thelma had sensed that something was "off" about her and expressed her concerns to the doctors. Right now though, she only wanted to spend time talking to her niece.

"You know, Sidney . . . a fellow named Tonio is on his way to see you. I e-mailed him yesterday. You must've made quite an impression for him to want to come all this way."

Maurice chuckled in the background. "Don't worry, Sidney, your aunt will do your hair nicely for when he arrives on Saturday. Just think thirty-six hours from now, he'll be here. The man sure doesn't waste any time. He must care about you a great deal."

"Kind of reminds me of you, sweetheart. Once you mustered your courage, there was no stopping you." She smiled at the man who made her life so happy. While Sidney had been away, they decided to elope. They had meant it to be a special surprise but that would have to wait.

The doctor came into the room just then, a look of confusion and concern on his face. "Hello, Thelma. Hello, Maurice. I have some questions to ask you. Did your niece have a boyfriend before going on her holidays?"

"Not as far as I knew." Thelma had no idea why he would ask that.

"Your niece is pregnant."

The doctor continued when there was no response except for stunned shocked. "She's about two and a half months along as far as I can tell. Do you know if she met anyone while she was on holiday that might be able to shed some light on the situation? The pregnancy itself could be detrimental to her health. We don't know if her body will be able to heal and support another life within her at the same time."

Maurice and Thelma both looked at him and said together, "Tonio!"

* * *

Tonio exited the plane, collected his luggage, and walked out of the airport. He hailed a cab that took him immediately to the hospital. He would check in to his room later. He felt an urgency to see Sidney first. He got to the hospital and was shown to her room by the head nurse. When he arrived, he was greeted by who he presumed to be, Aunt Thelma and new Uncle Maurice. He smiled kindly to them and let his glance slide over to the bed, taking in the sight of Sidney. He stopped midstride and stared at her. He knew things were bad, but nothing could have prepared him for the sight that he was beholding now. Her breathing machine with its own rhythm and all the wires and tubes were just too much for him to take in. He collapsed in the chair nearby with a scared look on his face. He seemed to try to recover himself and stood by Sidney's bedside. He put his hand on her head; the bandages had been removed along with the drainage tube a few weeks ago. He had stroked her hair in the past, and she'd always found it soothing. He started stroking her hair once again, hoping it would reach her wherever she was.

"It's a hard thing to take in all at once, I know," Thelma said, trying to be empathetic. "She's actually improved a little in the last couple of weeks. They had to do emergency surgery to release the pressure on her brain when they first brought her in. The drainage tube was removed two weeks ago. How did you come to know Sidney?"

"Well, actually, we met the first two weeks of her holiday. We were both staying at the same resort. I was on my honeymoon, by myself. That's a long unnecessary story to tell right now. She was alone as well, and we struck up a friendship," Tonio explained.

"You obviously struck up a hell of a lot more than that for you to be here now." Maurice piped up, a little agitated with the situation.

Thelma patted his knee and tried to sooth the atmosphere a bit. "Uh, we're just happy that you thought enough of our niece to come all this way."

Tonio bent his head and pressed a kiss to Sidney's forehead. He was overcome with sadness for her, and the tears started to spill over. He was usually able to keep his emotions in check, but seeing her like this was his undoing. Thelma went to him and rubbed his back as she handed him a Kleenex. "Why did this happen to her of all people? I know we didn't know each other long, but she's had a huge impact on my life. She was so happy and positive about most things. I was a better person for having known her, and I know it. How many people can say that? I just can't imagine her not being Sidney. What are the doctors saying about her recovery?"

"Well, that's where things get a little complicated. They don't know if or when she'll wake up. No one knows for sure how long she went without oxygen. So if she does wake up, only time will tell how much damage has been done," Thelma told him.

"It sounds like she's got a fifty-fifty chance," Tonio said, continuing to stroke her hair.

"There's more. Forgive me for asking, but did the two of you have relations?" Thelma didn't even blush. Tonio did. "Yes, we did. Why would you need to know such a thing?"

"Sidney is pregnant." There, she said it. She'd been dreading telling him, but he had a right to know the whole situation since he might be a father in the near future depending on what the doctors decided.

Tonio's mouth formed a silent O as he fought for the right thing to say. He hadn't seen this coming in a million years. She'd said she was on the pill, so he didn't give it a second thought. Now all thoughts went out of his mind entirely.

Just then, the doctor came in. "Is this the father?" Tonio just stared at him blankly as Thelma nodded her head. "We have a lot to talk about, sir. I'm sure Thelma has filled you in on what we know so far. If she continues to gain weight, then we will continue the pregnancy. Will you be responsible for the child if it's born while she's still in her coma?" the doctor asked directly.

There it was. Probably the biggest question someone had ever asked him in his whole life. At his age of thirty-two and with a stable career, he knew his answer immediately.

"Yes, without a doubt. I have a feeling I'll have lots of help." He turned shiny eyes upon Thelma and Maurice, who in turn took turns embracing him with joyous hugs.

What an unbelievable night. So much had changed in such a short amount of time. The unknown was a very real and terrifying threat that hung over all their heads and brought a sliver of fear down their spines despite their happiness over the recent events.

Now they just needed Sidney to wake up.

8

Tonio was invited over to Thelma and Maurice's for dinner on the fourth night. He was glad for the chance to get to know them a lot better since he was going to have some connection to them for the rest of his life.

He arrived at their place shortly before five with his bottle of wine tucked under his arm. He'd dressed semicasually, for it was Italy after all and still very hot. Their house was amazing with a picture-perfect postcard view of the ocean as far as the eyes could see. They had a wraparound deck, a hammock, and a cozy swing built for two. Below this, they had a nice-sized beach with a fire pit that was already set up for the night to come. Inside the house, the furnishings were modest yet exquisite. Whoever had decorated it had done a wonderful job. Real hardwood floors welcomed his warm feet with its coolness. The rooms were spacious enough with vaulted ceilings that led down to huge windows to let in enormous amounts of light. The kitchen had black granite countertops and state-of-the-art appliances. Thelma and Maurice were so happy with their home. How could they not be? Thelma and Maurice knew, after living in the city, how lucky they were.

Thelma opened the door and smiled at Tonio. "Welcome, Tonio. Please come and have a seat on the back deck. Can I bring you something to drink?"

With that, Tonio handed her the bottle of wine he'd brought with him. "I thought the least I could do was bring the wine."

"Thank you very much. I'll take it into the kitchen for Maurice to open. Just head on through those doors, we'll be out in a jiffy."

Tonio saw when he went out to the deck that it extended quite a ways. There was lots of room to suntan or host a large BBQ. It was ideal. He chose one of the recliners and waited for his hosts.

Thelma and Maurice didn't keep him waiting for long. They came out with three wine glasses, cheese spread with crackers, and pepperoni links. They too chose to sit in recliners. There was a feeling of closeness between the three of them. They had one very special person in common, and now it looked like there would be two if everything continued to go well.

"Thank you, Tonio, for coming tonight and for caring about Sidney the way you do. You're obviously a mature, honorable man to have handled things the way you have. You've seemingly taken everything in stride, considering the shock of the whole situation. I can only imagine what you might be feeling." Thelma reached over and patted his knee reassuringly.

"Well, I have to say, it's all come at me so fast. But one thing I do know is that I care for Sidney deeply. I have great respect for her. She too has been through a lot and came through it well. Now hopefully she'll come through this part too." Tonio looked longingly into his drink, suddenly very sad; he tried to shake it off.

"She's very strong, even now you know. She's stubborn too. These things should help her in coming around. Still, I just wish she would wake up. It's been so long now." Maurice commented. He too looked upset and reached for the bottle to refill their wine glasses. All three looked off into the distant sea. Each saying their own silent prayer for the return of the Sidney they once knew.

Tonio remembered how vibrant she had been, her laughter, like honey on your lips, sweet and welcoming. He remembered her running into the ocean without a care in the world, smiling back at him. He cursed and brushed the tears off his cheeks.

Thelma saw the raw agony on his tear-streaked face. She went to him then and embraced him in what she hoped was a comforting hug. He hugged her back. "I see where Sidney got her great hugs from now. She sure helped to cheer me up on the trip." Tonio cleared his throat and took a giant swallow of his wine, emptying it.

"If you don't mind me asking, what happened to you before you went on your honeymoon?" Thelma could hide her curiosity no more, not with the deck stacked.

Tonio went into the details of his Angelica experience. He didn't leave anything out, and to say the least, they both couldn't believe what he had gone through. For Thelma, it wasn't as bad as what she might have thought. He definitely had inner strength to come through it with such tenacity. Tonio credited Sidney with helping him see through those dark times. It wasn't hard to be happy around Sidney once he let himself. And in the end, he had hurt her by feeling more than both of them should have. And now she was in a coma in the hospital because he had left her. Well, he wouldn't leave her again unless she forced him to. And even if she only wanted to be friends, he would accept that.

Maurice got up to put the steaks on the BBQ. Thelma and Tonio continued to talk of his life. "So you're living in Greece right now to be near your mom, and your brother and his family are in New York. Will she be all right while you're here?"

"Mom is very independent. She likes to socialize with her friends a lot, so I think she won't miss me too much." Tonio smiled to himself. "Besides, it's nice to be back here again. If only the circumstances were a little different, I think I'd be having a great time. Now my whole world has turned upside down, and I could be a daddy. Wow, it's a lot of information to take. I've only been here four days. Just imagine the shock she's going to have when she wakes up. How do you think she'll take it?"

"Probably the same as you, shocked at first, and then hopefully she'll be as excited as we are all trying not to be. I personally don't want to get my hopes up just yet though I have to admit it's getting harder. I'm trying to stop myself from going to the nearest baby shop to buy cute little outfits." Thelma smiled at him; the excitement on her face was contagious. He smiled warmly back and then took a long sip of his wine.

"At least we have time on our side for now." Tonio stared at the ocean and thought of their sexually charged swim a few months ago. He felt himself getting overheated, and it had nothing to do with the warmth of the day.

"Would you mind telling me a little bit more about Sidney? What was she like as a child growing up?" Tonio wanted to know everything he could about her.

"Well, I really didn't see her all that much when she was young. We didn't live close to them at the time. But her mom always said what a bright girl she was, very bubbly and excited about life. She had a heart of gold and was usually a good girl, although I was told a couple of stories that confirmed she had a devilish streak to her." Thelma smiled at the memory's and continued on. "She had a lot of friends too, but she was never a follower. She had too much confidence for that. Her mom was the same way, so she came by it honestly. When her parents died though, I think a piece of her did too. She was never the same again after the accident. She stopped socializing as much and only kept in contact with a handful of people from that time in her life. I think she has a hard time trusting her heart to anyone after losing them. I know it was hard on us. I can only imagine how awful it must have been for her. For years now, up until a year ago when I met Maurice, it was just the two of us. There were many times I wished that she had had more of a father figure and loving mom to rely on. I did the best I could to stand in for them. I only hope they're happy with how she's turned out." Thelma looked pensive.

"From what I've seen and known of Sidney, I'd say you did a wonderful job." Tonio tried to reassure her. He sensed it was working when she lightheartedly changed the subject.

"How about we eat our steaks and potatoes out here and enjoy the view?" Aunt Thelma suggested.

"Sounds like a plan," Maurice said, coming out to set the table.

All three enjoyed the rest of the evening, trying to stay on safe subjects. They all knew that they were helpless to the circumstances of being brought together in such a fashion. Everything relied on Sidney and her ability to overcome the coma and support the life of their unborn child. They talked long into the night and emptied several bottles of wine. They all deserved to kick back and enjoy their beautiful surroundings without thinking of their worries for one night. They all knew they needed this time desperately.

"I was thinking, maybe you two could take the day off from the hospital tomorrow during the day. Take some time for yourselves, I'll stay with Sidney. It's been a while since you two had a break. Go sightseeing and see this beautiful country. In fact, I insist on it." Tonio tried to sound authoritative without being rude.

"Well, OK. If you're insisting, then I think we shall. Sound good to you, sweetie?" Thelma had a twinkle in her eyes, and Maurice knew all about that twinkle. It meant good times were on the horizon.

"That's fine by me." He smiled right back at his wife.

"Good, then it's settled. I'll see you two in the afternoon, then?"

"You bet, son." It was the first time Maurice had shown any real sense of affection to him, and it made him happy. *Things might be looking up*, he thought to himself.

FOREVER ITALY

9

Tonio arrived at the hospital around nine. He was still groggy from the night before, but it'd all been worth it. He went into Sidney's room, but nothing had changed; Sidney was still in her coma. He wondered what she was dreaming of this whole time. Was he in her thoughts somewhere? He guessed he'd probably never know. He opened her curtains to let the sun in and told her of his night with Thelma and Maurice.

"Thelma really loves you. She sang your praises all the way to the moon and back. She's very proud of you too. Their house is amazing. I can't wait for you to see it." Tonio could feel his throat tightening and felt the sting of tears. Was he just kidding himself that she would wake up? It had been almost two and a half months now. She was pregnant with a baby that may never know her or her loving touch.

He went to Sidney's side, his heart needing to be close to hers. Heart. He remembered being on the plane going home when he'd opened the present from her. The "Love Rock." He had been so touched; he'd almost gotten off the plane right there. But as he was high in the air at that particular moment, he decided against it.

He went to the side of her bed and leaned down close to her ear. Opening her hand, he pulled the "Love Rock" out of his pocket and placed it onto her palm. He closed her hand with his, stroked her hair with the other hand, and whispered in her ear, "I love you, Sidney, please come back to me." He wiped his tears away and looked down into her eyes.

All he could do was stare. Her eyes were open, looking right at him. "Sidney, Sidney? Sweetheart, can you hear me? Blink your eyes if you can." She blinked her eyes. "Oh my god! She's awake, she's awake, everybody!" Tonio pressed the call bell beside her bed, and the nurses came running. Suddenly there was a flurry of activity and excitement, every professional that was involved with her case came in to see her for themselves. Tonio stayed by her side the whole time, relishing in the fact that she was back.

Sidney couldn't talk while on the respirator, so they stuck to blinking once for *yes* and twice for *no*. Tonio continued talking to help soothe her in all the commotion.

"You're probably wondering how you and I got here. Well, you hit your head on the bottom of a pool. It wasn't deep enough for diving, so you banged your head on the bottom and lost consciousness. You've been asleep for a little while now. That's how you ended up here. Your aunt Thelma sent me an e-mail telling me what happened to you, and that's why I'm here now. You've been in a coma for the past two and a half months, and we've all been desperately waiting for you. Your aunt Thelma and uncle Maurice moved here to be close to you. You are truly loved, my sweet one." Tonio pressed a kiss to her forehead when he saw the tears rolling down her cheeks. "We don't know yet if there's anything wrong. It's just a wonder that you're even awake right now, so let's focus on the positive."

Time passed and eventually the doctors and nurses decided that she was stable enough to be left alone again.

Tonio took a deep breath and mustered all his courage to say the things he should have said before getting on that airplane months before. "I love you, Sidney, I should never have walked away from you. This is completely all my fault, and I want to spend the rest of my days making it up to you. I just hope you can forgive me for ever leaving your side." To his amazement, Sidney lifted her hand and placed the Love Rock to his cheek and smiled. He hoped it was her way of saying that she loved him too.

It was the most glorious day that Tonio could remember in a long time. He gently brushed her hair, and she closed her eyes, enjoying the feel of the soft bristles. Mostly, she genuinely cherished the fact the he loved her.

She couldn't believe that two months had passed. Two months that she could never get back. Suddenly she was terrified that something more might be wrong with her and tried to move her arms and legs. She was successful again in moving her hand up. Tonio's face was close to hers, and she cupped her palm against his baby-smooth cheek.

"It's all right, sweetheart, we'll have you strong again in no time," Tonio said, trying to sound reassuring. Tonio leaned down and gently pressed his soft lips to her cheek. It was a lingering promise of things to come, and he cherished her and these precious moments. He now fully understood how short life was.

"Oh my god! She's awake." Aunt Thelma stood in the doorway, dropped her bags, and rushed to her niece's bedside. She gently hugged and kissed Sidney until she was sure of what she was seeing and feeling. The excitement and shock overwhelmed her. "When did this happen? Why didn't the hospital call us?" Thelma took her hand and sat down next to her, tears freely falling down her cheeks.

"It doesn't matter, Thelma, she's back and that's all that counts." Maurice was all smiles and bent over Sidney to affectionately kiss her on the forehead.

"She awoke when I placed the Love Rock into her hand. I told her I loved her and wanted her to come back to me, and amazingly . . . she did. Then everyone came in, and it's been crazy in here up until an hour ago. The great news is that she can move her left arm and hand, which is the one that she writes with. Has anyone got a pen and paper? I'm sure she's got a lot of questions for us." Tonio looked at them expectantly.

Suddenly, Sidney smiled, obviously liking this idea. With unsteady fingers, Sidney wrote down her first question, "Ice chips?"

"I'm sure we can get that for you," Maurice said as he went off to get some ice from the machine down the hall.

"When can I go home?" was her next question. Tonio and Aunt Thelma exchanged glances; neither was quick to offer up a response. "Well, from what we know, the doctors will have to assess you every day. You'll get stronger as time goes on. We'll just have to be patient. It might take a while for your body to adjust to your new circumstances." Aunt Thelma gave her a reassuring pat on her hand.

"Here's your ice chips, dear." Maurice handed it over to Tonio who accepted the small cup. Gently, placing the ice across her lips, the ice melted on her hot lips. They shared a caressing moment with their eyes, both longing for it to be more.

"We don't want to rush anything. They have the best doctors here and all the specialists that you might need. As long as you stay in the hospital, your health will be taken care of more quickly than if you were having services outside of your home." Maurice offered up for conversation. He was worried that Sidney might try to rush her recovery.

Maurice made sense; she knew this. But she couldn't shake the feeling that there was more to it than what they were telling her. It was all just too much to take in at the moment. She just wanted to sleep and have this whole nightmare behind her and go back to her regular life. With only one change, she wanted Tonio to move back with her. She loved him too.

She wrote down that she wanted to sleep, and they respected her wishes and left her room to congregate outside her closed hospital room door.

"Can you believe it? Holy cow! I can't even say how happy I am." Thelma embraced Tonio and Maurice excitedly; tears were rolling down her cheeks.

For the next couple of days, they worked out a schedule. One of them at all times would be by her side. By appearances, she was taking the whole thing in her own stride. She wasn't able to move her legs just yet, but her right hand was starting to function. She could pick up a pen, and all the doctors were happy with her progress so far.

No one dared to mention the pregnancy. They all agreed she was mentally too fragile to handle information of this magnitude. Everyone knew that the secret had to come out soon as she was starting to show. She had lost weight over that last two months, and her round belly would soon give it all away.

She had a lot of questions for the doctors who were only too happy that she had them to ask at all. They informed Sidney that she was under the water long enough to have suffered severe neurological damage. In their professional opinion, she was a lucky young lady.

It was on the fifth day after her awakening that she was taken off the respirator. After a successful twenty-four hours of breathing well on her own, she asked for the one thing that she wanted the most since awakening, a bath.

Luckily for Tonio, it was on his shift that this request was brought to life. The bath was drawn, and the nurses gently placed her into the tub with the body sling. The calm water caressed her skin and made her feel very alive. She'd anticipated the tingling sensation of the warm water on her skin. Tonio poured water from the jug onto her scalp; a small moan escaped her lips as she tilted her head back and savored every luxurious moment.

Her voice was also coming back to her. Sure, it was raspy and small, but at least it was one more thing to check off her recovery list.

Tonio heard her say something and leaned in to hear her better. "I've gotten fat with all the tube feeding," Sidney commented while rubbing her belly. "I'm going to get on the treadmill as soon as I can." She smiled up into Tonio's pale face. "What is it? What's wrong?"

"Nothing, Sidney, I just think we should take it slow. Everything's going to happen in its own time."

"OK. But you know what a fanatic I am about my exercise." Sidney continued to rub her belly.

If only I could tell her, Tonio thought. *This just isn't the right time or place.*

To keep his hands and mind occupied, he reached for the washcloth and soap and proceeded to wash her body. Her breasts had started to swell with her hormone levels; the books he was reading on the subject were making him aware of her developing pregnancy, making it a more intimate experience for him. If only he could share his thoughts with her. He was feeling ashamed of himself for withholding such important thoughts.

"Don't forget my back. I think my front's clean enough by now!" Sidney hoarsely laughed up at him, enjoying the soothing attention. She wasn't feeling well enough to even take her thoughts to a sexual level. It took all her strength just to sit up right in the tub, and her throat was bothering her from the ventilator tube.

Sidney was as happy as could be after her wonderful bath; she was ever thankful to Tonio. Who could imagine that their lives would end up so entwined with one another. When they had parted company before the accident, she knew in all eventualities they would come together again. She would've made it happen. He'd saved her without her even knowing that she was falling. She'd been searching for the empty space in her heart to be filled since her parents had passed away. She didn't even realize how empty that space in her heart was until she met Tonio. He'd filled up the whole void like a broken locket being pieced back together again. Her life was with him, and she couldn't wait to get out of the hospital to start it.

She loved him. Oh, of this she was certain.

There was a weird feeling inside her; she could feel it. Something was different. But try as she might to figure it out, she just couldn't put her finger on it. All she wanted now was to get back home and on with her new life with just her and Tonio.

10

Another week went by and Sidney was growing stronger every day. She was now starting to eat soft foods, ice cream, and nonacidic drinks so as not to reirritate her throat. She could now move all her limbs, slowly, mind you; but she was very happy to be on the mend. The doctors were surprised to see her quick recovery and now optimistic of an early discharge. She had physiotherapy coming in daily to help strengthen her limbs, and every day promised to be one more closer to getting home.

Aunt Thelma, Maurice, and Tonio had asked the doctors to not tell her about the little life growing inside of her just yet. All were concerned of her present state of mind. They wanted her to be physically strong enough to handle the news. It just seemed the right thing to do for Sidney's sake. When the time was right, they would tell her.

It was on her second to last day in the hospital that she received a visitor. "Welcome back!"

Sidney looked up from her magazine. "Oh my god! Is it really you?"

Marcos, with all his charm, presented himself at her bedside and pressed light kisses to both cheeks. "Of course. I heard that you were feeling better after waking up from your coma. I had to see for myself. I came as soon as I heard."

"I'm so glad you did." Sidney put her hand on Tonio's arm, so happy to see her new friend again. "They told me that you were the one who found me in the pool. Thank you for saving my life, Marcos. If there's ever any way that I can repay you . . . just let me know. I know I probably won't even come close to what you've done for me, but I can at least try, can't I?"

"Don't even give it another thought. So when do you get out?" he asked, placing his hands casually into his pockets.

"They're saying tomorrow. I can't wait. I'm so tired of hospital food and this hard uncomfortable bed. Besides, I came here to see the countryside, not the same four walls day in and day out of a hospital room. Do you have any idea how many magazines, crossword puzzles, and books I've read?"

"Then I shall entertain you until your family shows up. Then I'm off to a business meeting. So how are you really?" Marcos's concern was evident all over his face. She enjoyed these sincere qualities in him.

"Well, firstly, I've fallen in love. Second, I love this country, and third, I feel very grateful that I'm still here in one piece to enjoy it. I used to think that life was all about work. My life was extremely hectic, flying from one state to the next, never pausing long enough to really enjoy it all. I was so busy running around the parks instead of just going for a sauntering stroll through them. Do you know what I mean?"

"I went on a visit to your place of the world a short time ago. I could literally sense the people's stress as they walked by me on the street. Their faces were so drawn. Most of them didn't seem to be overflowing with happiness. I don't like to generalize, but those are my impressions on what I saw there. Here, this is my home for many reasons. But the true reason is because I can breathe and be at peace with myself. I love walking the vineyards early in the morning, inhaling the aroma of the sweet vines. There is nothing like this place anywhere in the world."

"Wow, you've got it bad! It must be nice to be truly in love with the place you live. I can't say that I had those feelings toward New York, but then I never stopped working long enough to really think about it."

Sidney thought about their conversation long after Marcos left. For some reason, it really bothered her. Maybe she was just jealous. Or maybe it was the feeling that she had missed out on something along the way. She'd thought that she was happy in her life, but now she was second guessing herself. How could this happen? She'd always been so sure of herself and her choices.

It gave her a lot to think about. She still had some time before she headed back to the States.

Time, she couldn't believe how much of it had been lost. Two months of her life were gone, never to be returned to her. Maybe this event in her life was just what she needed. *I can't go back*, she thought. *I just want to press onward and maybe make a few changes. Would I really be happy if I just happened to stay here? And what about Tonio?* She pressed her lips together and hung her head. She was tired and decided to get ready for bed. It was all just too much excitement for her. Tomorrow she would think more seriously about her next step.

The next day, she was released. Aunt Thelma, Maurice, and Tonio were there to help celebrate the wonderful day. The weather was wonderful, and she thoroughly enjoyed the scenic drive back to Maurice and Aunt Thelma's new home.

Tonio sat with her in the back and held her hand happily. "What are you thinking?"

"It just seems so surreal. I'm here with you and my family on our way to their new home in Italy. It's wonderful." Sidney grimaced a little, her smile fading.

"What is it? Where are you hurting?" There was a little edge to Tonio's voice as he looked her over with great concern.

"I just feel so sick to my stomach. It must be the windy road. It's been a long time since I was in a vehicle you know. I'll feel better once I have a drink and just sit down for a while," Sidney said, rubbing her belly.

Maurice glanced at Tonio in the rearview mirror, a question in his eyes. *He's got to tell her soon, he just has to.* Maurice and Thelma had talked long into the night the evening before. All thought it would be best if Tonio was the one to tell her; after all, he was the father to be. They really liked Tonio. The only problem they had with him was that he lived in Greece. Just how the heck was this supposed to work out? They knew that he had his mother there and probably wouldn't leave her. Or would he? All they knew was that he thought the world of her and she of him. The two of them were their own little family. Would she accept Sidney and her baby even though her son and Sidney had only known each other for three months and weren't married or living near one another? There were so many problems that had no solutions to them yet.

They themselves weren't planning on leaving Italy. They had fallen in love with their life here. They hadn't broken the news to Sidney yet. Honestly, they were fearful of her reaction. With the baby on the way, Sidney would need them more than ever. Thelma knew that she and Maurice were being selfish, but these were their "golden years," and she wanted to spend them the way they wanted. Thelma just couldn't believe how much her life had changed in the last year; it was now completely unrecognizable. She herself felt different, more alive and happier than she'd ever been.

Maurice pulled the SUV up in front of their new home. Sidney was taken aback by the size of it. She absolutely loved the old stonework and the sedate grandeur of it all. "It's so beautiful here. I guess I won't have to worry about being right under your feet."

"No, you won't. We've made the room on the other side of the house yours so as not to disturb you. Maurice is an early riser you know." Aunt Thelma patted Maurice's leg.

"Well, if she wakes to the smell of fresh coffee brewing, I wouldn't mind the company. The sunrises are glorious." Maurice's invitation was sincere. He would like the opportunity to get to know his new niece a bit better.

"She can't have coffee. It's got caffeine in it," Aunt Thelma said while helping Sidney with her bags down the hall to her room.

"What are you talking about? I always have coffee in the morning." Sidney would've asked more questions, but she was quickly diverted by the view out of her bedroom window. Suddenly, coffee wasn't on her mind at all.

Seeing that she had been thankfully rescued by their surroundings, Aunt Thelma busied herself with straightening the bed sheets, which were perfectly fine before.

"Holy cow! I don't think I'll ever want to leave this room." Sidney gasped.

Aunt Thelma walked over to the double doors and opened them wide. She and Sidney walked out on to the huge deck, which joined up with the main one overlooking the ocean. Sidney walked toward the rail and leaned on it. Closing her eyes, she inhaled the gentle breeze that caressed her skin. She thought to herself, *How amazing is this?*

Maurice and Tonio came out on the deck from the living room doors and placed a jug of ice tea on the patio table. Maurice motioned for them to come and join them.

Sidney sat down and looked at the ice tea. "Don't you want to have some wine?" Sidney asked Tonio with a sexy glint in her eyes, remembering their times on the beach together.

Tonio caught the meaning in her eyes. "I think we ought to have something different, more refreshing. At least for now." Tonio quickly averted his eyes to the water, not daring to keep eye contact. His heart was pounding. He needed to tell her the truth; he was just waiting for the right moment.

Sidney was taken aback at his coolness. Were his feelings for her changing? What had she done wrong? Sidney tried to lighten the mood. "So when are we heading back to the States?"

Suddenly, all three of them looked preoccupied with their own thoughts; no one dared to answer her. "Hello! Did anyone hear me? What are the plans for going back home? Answer me please!"

Aunt Thelma cleared her throat and thought to herself, *No time like the present.*

"Well, dear, Maurice and I have decided that we're not going back." Aunt Thelma waited for her response to come and was sitting on the edge of her chair, hands clasped together in her lap, looking anxious.

"You're what? You're staying?" Sidney couldn't say that she wasn't surprised.

"As you can see," she waved her hand toward the ocean, "we have our own little piece of paradise here. We would be fools to leave it now. I've worked hard all my life ever dreaming that one day I could be fortunate enough to live in a place such as this. We're staying." Thelma waited for her niece to say something, anything.

Sidney just sat there, paused, and then carefully chose her words.

"Well. I have some news for you too. I'm also staying. When Marcos visited me the other day, he made me really think of what I wanted out of my life. I realized that I was simply floating through and never really touching the ground.

Some of the best times of my life have been on this trip. So like you, I'm staying too." Sidney got up to meet her aunt halfway for a huge hug. All were laughing and smiling. There was a sense of relief in the air, and the happiness that the three of them felt was profound.

'There's more . . . while you were away Maurice and I eloped. I hope your not mad, we just simply didn't want to wait any longer." Thelma waited for her response.

"How could I be mad? That's wonderful, congratulations!" The four embraced again with genuine happiness for the newly weds.

* * *

Later in the evening after dinner and Aunt Thelma and Maurice had gone to bed, Tonio and Sidney went for a walk together on the beach. The moon was out in full strength, lighting their way along the sand. Tonio stopped in his tracks and grabbed Sidney's hand, bringing her up softly against his body. Leaning in, his lips descended onto hers. It started out luxuriously tantalizing and then delved into an insatiable hunger, leaving both of them shuddering for breath. Sidney put her head on his shoulder to get her bearings again. Then she looked up to stare into his eyes. "Well, I guess that answers my question."

"And what question would that be?" Tonio asked, holding her close.

"If you still wanted me or not, if you still loved me the same way."

"If I ever made you doubt me, then I'm sorry. There's been a lot going on lately, and everyone is making huge decisions right now. I have a lot on my mind too." Tonio kissed her again to stop her from asking what that was. He knew in his heart that this was not the right time for that question. But it was the right time for a different one.

Suddenly, Tonio bent down onto one knee and opened his hand, revealing an engagement ring that had heart-shaped emeralds on both sides of a diamond with white gold. It was an engagement ring.

"Sidney, my love for you is so complete. You may think that I'm crazy for asking you to marry me, but I can't think of one reason why I shouldn't. I've never believed in love at first sight before I met you. I want to be with you forever, no matter what happens. Will you marry me?"

Sidney was in tears by the time he'd finished his proposal. "Yes, yes. A thousand times, YES!" Sidney barreled into Tonio's arms, knocking them both down onto the sand.

Tonio felt the warm tears from her eyes falling down onto his cheeks and held her to him. He never wanted to let her go again. And he never would. Suddenly, their clothes were no longer on them. They just couldn't get enough of each other. Sidney grabbed his hand and placed it on her swollen breast. Suddenly feeling pain, Sidney brought her head up sharply. Then Tonio was kissing her stomach and down to her thighs, bringing wave after wave of sensation. She hadn't felt like this in a long time. Their lovemaking was wonderfully sweet, soft, and sensual. Neither one wanted to hurry. The stars exploded behind their closed eyes, and they drifted off to sleep in each other's arms.

Tonio woke up a half hour later. Trying not to wake her, he gently picked her up in his strong arms and carried her back to the house. Cautiously, he laid her on the bed and undressed them both. Then he joined her in bed. Sensing his nearness, Sidney snuggled in close to him. Tonio gave a sigh of contentment, and Sidney nuzzled deeper into his chest.

FOREVER ITALY

11

Sidney and Tonio met Aunt Thelma and Maurice in the kitchen for breakfast the next morning. "I was just about to give up on the two of you. You're just in time for hash browns, toast, and eggs . . . I hope you're hungry," Aunt Thelma stated.

"Mmm, I could clearly smell everything all the way down to my room. Delicious. As far as being hungry goes, I'm starving," Sidney said, rubbing her belly.

The rest of them exchanged side-glances. Aunt Thelma, in particular, gave Tonio a hard stare. He winked at her. She sucked her breath in quickly and stiffened her back with indignation. *What was that all about?* she wondered.

"Sidney and I would like to talk to you. Please, Thelma, have a seat." Tonio gestured toward her nearby chair.

After she was comfortably seated with breakfast on the table, Tonio and Sidney spilled the beans.

"Sidney and I are getting married." Tonio's smile went from one ear to the next.

Aunt Thelma dropped her spoon into her coffee cup. "Ohhhh, well, isn't that just wonderful news!"

All four embraced and congratulated one another. Then they started to eat their breakfast.

Aunt Thelma brought the coffee cup halfway to her mouth and paused, lost in her own thoughts.

"Aunt Thelma, what's on your mind? You seem far away. You are happy for us, aren't you?"

Thelma looked up, startled. "Of course I am, honey. I just hope you two aren't rushing into this. You've only known each other for a short amount of time."

Sidney was hurt that her aunt thought so little of her personal judgment. Putting her hand on Tonio's, she charged on. "That's the pot calling the kettle black. Look at you and Maurice. You two waited a little longer to be engaged but not that long. I love Tonio, and I know that he loves me. That's the end of it. Besides, I didn't question you when you and Maurice got engaged! Why can't you just be happy for me?" Tears were now rolling down her cheeks.

"I just don't want to see you make a rash decision in your special condition." Aunt Thelma tried to soften her words with a smile.

It didn't work. "Well, that's just it, isn't it? It's my rash decision to make, not yours. I'm feeling happier than I've ever felt. Why can't you just support me?"

Aunt Thelma went to the counter to grab some Kleenex for her niece.

Tonio was enraged. Here was their special moment. How dare she ruin it for them? "I think I've heard enough of this nonsense. Look, sometimes in life things happen unexpectedly for the right reasons. When I'm with Sidney, I feel alive. How could that ever be wrong?"

Maurice, who had sat quietly watching the events unfold thought it was time for his two cents. "I support you two, no matter what happens." He looked pointedly at his wife. "Your aunt and I wish you every happiness, don't we, Thelma?"

"Absolutely."

Sidney had never been happier in her life. So many changes in such a short amount of time and now she was getting married. She'd never thought three months ago that she would be living in Italy and marrying a handsome Greek man. *Amazing*, she thought with glowing cheeks and tear-filled eyes.

Sidney excused herself to go and jump into the shower. Aunt Thelma and Maurice used this opportunity to have a little chat with Tonio.

"Firstly, welcome to the family, Tonio. Secondly, aren't you forgetting to mention something to her, like . . . a baby?" Aunt Thelma couldn't help the anger in her voice.

Tonio was a bit taken aback by her candid emotion. "I'm telling her tonight. I was hoping that we could spend some time together first, you know reconnect with each other. So then, when I told her about the baby, she might feel more comfortable with it and me. I just wanted her to know that I really wanted to marry her firstly because I love her and not just because she's having my baby."

"I see. Don't you think it might have the opposite effect." Thelma looked at him skeptically. "She might think that you tricked her into marrying you."

"I see your point. I would hope that she'd know my intentions are sincere. I'd like to think that she knows me better than that. Anyway, could I treat the two of you to dinner tonight to have her alone here? It's not the sort of thing that I want to spring on her in a public setting. I want her honest reaction."

"Oh, I think you'll definitely get that!" replied Thelma.

"You don't think she'll be happy?"

"It's hard to say at this point. She'll be shocked that's for sure. OK, Tonio, we'll go out for dinner tonight. But don't expect us to stay out late. If this goes badly, she'll be needing us too."

Tonio nodded his head. Then he reached out and embraced Thelma. "Thank you for trusting me with your niece. I'll do everything I can to make her happy and our child."

Maurice shook his hand and gave him a knowing look. "We know you will."

Tonio sent Sidney out for a walk on the beach so that he'd have time to set everything up. He knew he'd only have one chance at making this special for her. He was so nervous. What if she went into hysterics? Or worse yet, if she walked out on him altogether?

Trying to set these thoughts aside, he busied himself with lighting candles on the deck, in the kitchen, and living room. From outside, he could hear the soft music playing in the background. He'd made them steak and lobster for dinner, romantic and full of protein for the two of them.

"Well, well. What's all this about? Everything looks amazing, Tonio!" Sidney went up to Tonio and embraced his back while he worked at the stove. The lobster in the pot was done and ready.

"Would you mind waiting for dinner to be served outside on the deck? Your drink is on the table."

"Sure, honey. Hey, that's the first time I've called you that. Sounds good, doesn't it?"

"Wonderful, sweetheart." Tonio smiled down into her eyes and gave her the sweetest of kisses before gently patting her on the rump to send her off outside.

Ten minutes later, he had everything laid out on the table. He'd also added a caesar salad and baked potatoes to the menu. It all looked delicious, and Sidney was starving, as usual—a fact that she'd not caught on to just yet. To her, everything was a side effect of being in the coma.

They ate their meal in companionable company. Both were so happy to be together starting their lives, and nothing else mattered to them.

"I guess I'll have to quit my job and start all over again here. I don't think it'll be that easy, but at least I have a lot of experience," Sidney said, thinking out loud.

"You might be surprised. Your skills are honed and well-rounded for the market. I think any company who hires you will be lucky. I've already looked into doing some writing for the travel brochure companies here. I think between the two of us, we'll be OK." Tonio gave Sidney what he hoped was a reassuring smile.

Sidney felt Tonio's leg brush up against hers under the table. It sent little shivers up her spine.

The candles shimmered rusty colors onto their tanned skin, causing shadows of light and dark to dance across their faces. The wind was only a slight breeze, and in the distance, waves were cresting and falling onto the shore. It was beyond romantic. They shared conversations of dreams for their future. The lovely painting in their minds of what was to come. Tonio wanted her to eat most of her dinner first before he told her of the baby. He wanted her well nourished now, in case she couldn't eat later.

After they'd finished their dinner, Tonio went inside for their dessert. He'd made a cake for her earlier when she'd been napping. It was a chocolate raspberry layered cake with delicious icing on top. Next, he put sparklers into it and lit them. When he approached Sidney, she gave a glorious noise from somewhere deep in her throat.

"Wow, is every night going to be this magical?"

"We can try." Tonio grinned at her.

Tonio set his creation down and cut her a piece. He waited till she was halfway through and then . . .

"I have something that I want to tell you, Sidney. It's very important to you and our lives ahead. I want you to clearly understand that I want to marry you no matter what happens. Loving you has been the best thing to ever happen to me, bar none."

"Relax, Tonio, you're sweating. Nothing could be this serious. Believe me, whatever you could have to tell me isn't worth all this seriousness." Sidney covered his hand with hers and gently squeezed.

"Sidney, we're having a baby." There, he'd said it.

"Come again?" Sidney screwed up her face, not understanding. She withdrew her hand from his.

"You're pregnant."

"What in the devil are you talking about? How?" Sidney was shocked. She dropped her fork, and it rattled loudly against her plate as it landed.

"The night of the boat cruise? Well, that's when the doctors believe we conceived. It's the only time that we were together intimately."

Sidney's emotions were welling up inside of her, her anger almost boiling over. "I've been out of my coma for the past week, and no one told me? The three of you knew this the whole time . . . how could you NOT tell me? I'm only the mother!" Her anger was all consuming. Then she stood up and threw the rest of her drink in his face. As she ran away from him into the house, he thought he heard her calling him an asshole. Or at least something close to it.

He didn't dare follow her in. While mopping up his face, she'd given him the distinct impression that she needed some time alone.

12

Unbelievable bastard. How could he do this to me? Pregnant . . . me? I'm now over three months, so even if I wanted to do something about it, I can't. My choice has been taken away. Unbelievable! Sidney sat down on the edge of her bed and laid her head in her hands. "It's just too much. I can't process this much all at once. One day engaged, the other, pregnant. Who lives their lives this way!" she yelled at the empty room. She was just so damn angry at them all.

How dare them take the choice away from me. She didn't even know if she wanted to have kids in the first place. Now it didn't even matter what she wanted. She was pregnant, and motherhood was on the horizon. *Well, at least I have some time to get used to the idea, seven months in fact.*

She hoped that once her anger settled down, she would feel a little differently. Right now, she was terrified. *What happens now? I guess that I'll make a doctor's appointment soon, make sure the little one's all right.* Suddenly it hit her. No wonder no one had wanted her to drink alcohol or have caffeine. Her breasts were so tender, and she could smell everything in sight or out. It also explained why she'd been feeling under the weather lately. She also wondered why the doctors hadn't told her of the baby. She had a lot of unanswered questions, but Tonio was the last person she wanted to talk to at the moment.

He tried to trick me into marrying him. I guess it's safe to assume that he wants this baby. The thought of Tonio wanting the baby softened her resolved a little, but not much.

There was a gentle knock at the door. "It's Aunt Thelma, honey, can I please come in and talk to you? I know you're mad, and you have every right to be."

Sidney unlocked the door and held it open for her aunt to enter. "Just what in the devil inspired you to keep this baby news from me?" Sidney asked as she closed the door and placed her hands on her hips. "I never thought in a million years that you, above all people, would betray me this way." Tears of anger descended on her cheeks, and she quickly brushed them away.

Aunt Thelma tried to hug her; Sidney brushed her away. "No, that's not going to work this time."

"Listen to me, Sid, I know that you're very mad and hurt. Please let me explain. After I'm done, then you can pass judgment on me, but not until then. OK?" She searched her niece's eyes imploringly.

"You'd better hurry before I won't talk to you too."

"We found out when you were in the coma, obviously. Then Tonio came to see you and never left. He wanted us to keep it quiet so that he could tell you when the timing was right."

"So the timing was right when I no longer had a choice in the matter. Even though it affects my entire life? That doesn't make sense."

"We all assumed that you would be happy and go on with your life being a mom. Were we wrong?"

Sidney went and sat on her bed; Aunt Thelma followed suit. Sidney folded her hands in her lap and played with her fingers. "I don't honestly know. Perhaps if it had been my idea in the first place, I would be excited. All I feel now is cheated by the ones that supposedly love me the most. How would you expect me to feel?"

"Look, Sidney, when you came into my life, I didn't have a choice either. Not that I regret anything because I don't. But life throws things at you constantly that you don't expect, but usually through all the dark uncertainty, there are many rays of sunlight and happiness. It's the unexpected things, my dear, that make everything worth it. No matter how bad things get. I think and hope that once you get over your shock, you'll be seeing things in a whole new light." Aunt Thelma then reached over and gave her niece a long warm hug.

Sidney felt herself succumb to her aunt's heartfelt words. And the hug didn't hurt either.

"I just need some time to get over the shock and get used to this. I don't want to see Tonio right now under any circumstances. He lied to me."

"I did nothing of the sort, Sidney," Tonio said, opening her door. "I just didn't tell you everything right away."

Sidney's face flushed with temper. *How dare he!*

Seeing that it was her time to exit, Aunt Thelma hurriedly left the room, leaving the two of them to hash it out. *It's probably just what they need anyway,* she thought.

"How do you call not telling me about our unborn child, not lying to me?"

"Look, I didn't tell you at the beginning because you were under so much stress. It was the doctor's idea in the first place not to tell you for that reason alone. So I thought a little longer couldn't hurt. Besides, I thought you would be happy about the baby when you did find out. But apparently, that's not the case," Tonio said, gazing down sadly at the ground.

"I just feel that if you could keep this from me, what else are you hiding?"

"Come on now, Sidney, you know me better than that. I thought you knew who I was." Tonio was beside himself. This was not the way he'd wanted things to go. He now felt very foolish.

Sidney mustered her courage. "I want you to go away, Tonio, and don't come back. I don't know if I can ever forgive you for this. Please, just go!" When he didn't leave immediately, she herself ran from the room.

Tonio just stood there. He could hear the quiet around him and Sidney sobbing from somewhere in the house. He hung his head, feeling like the life had been drawn completely out of him. He walked to the front door, closing it quietly behind him.

Sidney collapsed into her aunt's arms. Her heart was breaking, and the betrayal that she felt was wounding her deeply. She didn't want to be in her aunt's arms. She was an accomplice, the enemy. But realizing she didn't have many options open to her at the moment, she gave herself permission to emotionally let go. Aunt Thelma had been like a mother to her, and she knew that she'd never do anything to intentionally hurt her.

"Sidney, I know your upset, sweetie. I think you're just too upset to listen to reason at the moment. Hear this, Tonio loves you. He wanted you to know that he wanted to marry you before you knew about the baby. He honestly was not trying to trick you into anything. He still wants to marry you. Please try to think clearly." Aunt Thelma squeezed her niece tightly against her. "Don't turn your back on someone who had the best intentions toward you."

Sidney didn't respond. All she wanted was to process the last forty-eight hours alone in her room. She thanked her aunt and walked somberly down the hallway.

Her aunt watched her go, shaking her head in dismay. How life had changed for them all.

The next morning, she was up early to the fresh smell of coffee brewing. She got out of bed and put her robe on. She went into the kitchen and poured her last cup of coffee for a long time to come. She figured one more couldn't hurt. On the deck, she spied Maurice and went to join him.

"Well, you're up early, couldn't sleep?" Maurice saw her full coffee cup, then saw her puffy eyes and decided to let it go. Some things just weren't worth fighting about.

"I have too much on my mind these days."

Maurice reached over and patted her knee. "You'll figure it out."

"What, no speeches?" Sidney was happy he wasn't trying to make her feel better by partaking in a lot of goodwilled advice.

"You're old enough to decide what and who you want in your life. It's not up to me to tell you what to do. You can figure it out just fine on your own. You know we support you no matter what, so you'll let us know what you decide either way."

Sidney smiled at him. "Thanks, Maurice."

13

Two days went by, and Sidney was becoming stir-crazy. She wanted to get out and see the Italy she had planned on before her accident. Her aunt decided that she should go out, so she made arrangements for Sidney to visit one of the vineyards. The catch was that she wouldn't tell her which one, in exchange for going out. Sidney reluctantly agreed, just happy to do something else.

The cab arrived and Aunt Thelma gave discreet directions to the driver. Sidney relaxed in the backseat and watched the ocean and countryside go by. She breathed in the fresh crisp air. They rounded a corner, and suddenly Sidney knew which winery her aunt had made plans at.

Marcos stood there with a smug smile on his face, awaiting her arrival.

Sidney got out of the car and hugged him. She had always enjoyed his personality, and they got on well together. "Well, well. Boy, my aunt sure is batting a hundred with this surprise. How are you, Marcos?"

"Very well, thank you. And you?" Marcos asked, holding her at arms length, taking a long look at her.

"Angry, confused, scared. I'm pregnant, Marcos."

Marcos looked at her with shock and then was immediately hugging her again in congratulations.

"I don't know what I'm going to do, Marcos."

"Let me give you a tour around the vineyard. I guarantee that by the end of your time here, you'll know your path in life."

Liking his playfulness, she laughed. *Like spending a day at this vineyard will solve anything for me*, she thought sarcastically.

"Come, I want to show you around my land."

Sidney followed Marcos to a nearby cart and boarded it. They went all around the vineyard. Marcos explained the ins and outs of the business to her. Knowing that she had been heavily involved with the marketing aspects of business, he picked her brain, looking for new ideas and potential markets. She was only too happy to oblige him, and by the end of the tour, he had some new potentially wealthy ideas to bring to their next meeting.

It had grown late in the day, and Marcos invited her to stay for dinner.

He showed her to one of the guest rooms to freshen up. It was a novelty room shaped like a cave, having rock walls and a waterfall that doubled as a shower. It was lit by candlelight and was very romantic. The sound of the water flowing over and landing gently echoed against the walls.

There was a knock at her door, and she went to answer it. She was beside herself when she realized who her guest was. It was Tonio!

"Are you just going to stand there, staring at me? Or are you going to invite me in?" Sidney went to shut the door, and Tonio put his hand against it and pushed it open wider to allow the cart with food to enter.

"I don't know what you're doing here, Tonio, but I'm not ready to talk yet."

"Please, Sidney, for our child's sake, just hear me out."

He took her hand and walked her over toward the bed. When they were both sitting, he spoke, "I know you think I've tricked you, that I lied to you. That was never my intention. I just wanted you to be ready to hear the truth. I'm truly sorry for the way things have worked out."

She could tell by the strength and conviction in his voice that he meant every word. Somewhere in the heart of her, her resolve started to melt. She could also see the glint of tears in his eyes as he continued on.

"It's just this simple. I want you in my life, Sidney. I've had a long time to think about my feelings. I love you now and always will. I'll take care of you and the baby, please don't give up on us because of a misunderstanding?"

By now both of them were crying, both in agony of their feelings for each other. He reached for her then. Cupping her wet cheek in his hand, their lips met with such sweet pleasure. Sidney couldn't hide her feelings anymore. She moaned aloud when the kiss went deeper. Before they lost all control, she pulled back. Searching his eyes, she saw what she needed to see. "I love you too, Tonio. I'm so sorry for the way I've reacted. It was all just too much news at once. I want this baby. As for marrying you . . . does next month work?"

Between kissing, hugging, tears of laughter and happiness, he responded, "Yes, my darling. Absolutely, yes. Now how about we eat? We've got to fatten you up."

That night, they sincerely made love to one another. Content in their relationship and their future together, all boundaries were eradicated. They were both beyond happy, and their tender lovemaking proved it.

At nine in the morning, there was a knock at the door. Tonio went to answer it.

"Good morning, my friends." It was Marcos.

"Wait, you two know each other?" Sidney was confused.

"Of course we do. I give out brochures of his vineyard to my clients on their way to Italy. It works out well. Sometimes I even get some free wine." Tonio clapped Marcos on the shoulder.

"How come you didn't say anything before now."

"The subject just never came up," Tonio replied lazily.

Marcos cleared his throat. "Would you two please join me for breakfast? I have something I want to talk to you about."

They were very curious and accepted the invitation without delay. "Give us twenty minutes to freshen up." Sidney, who still didn't have any clothes on, hugged the bedsheet close to her.

Marcos winked at her. "No hurry, you just take your time."

She and Tonio showered playfully together, each taking a turn with the soap and washing each other's backs. It was so nice to be comfortable with someone like this. She didn't even feel the urge to run away. Her life had never been so complicated, but yet she was relishing all of it.

The breakfast table was huge, just like the room it was situated in. It was covered in fruit, sausages, rolls, coffee, orange juice, eggs, and toast. Sidney noticed an older gentleman seated next to Marcos who she definitely thought was his father. The family resemblance was uncanny. At least Marcos knew that he was going to be just as handsome when he too got older.

Marcos motioned for them to sit down. "Please be seated. We have much to discuss."

"Please meet my father, Eros. Papa, these people are the ones I was telling you about. This is Sidney and Tonio."

"It's nice to meet you." He held out his hand for them to shake it.

Whatever this is about must be pretty big, Sidney thought to herself.

Only when their plates were loaded with food did the conversation really get going.

"Do you have any plans to return to the city, Sidney?" Marcos asked pointedly.

"Actually, I've decided to stay here in Italy, marry Tonio, and have our baby. As you can tell, things have a way of changing quickly. I hadn't really thought about work just yet. Too many other things have been on my mind." She turned to Tonio and smiled. She was in awe of what she'd just said. Was it really her life she was talking about?

"What about you, Tonio?"

"Why do you ask?" Tonio wanted to flip the table a bit and find out what their angle was.

"My father and I were brainstorming some ideas. Sidney, we would like to hire you as head of our marketing department. We have a new opening, and since you have an excellent background, well . . . I think we have to jump at an opportunity such as this."

Sidney, who had just bitten off a piece of toast, stopped chewing. She looked back and forth from Marcos to Tonio and to his father and then back again. "Me?" She quickly chewed the rest and gulped down some orange juice.

"We will equal your previous pay plus a 5 percent increase a year, with a cap of course. Plus, medical and dental which might come in pretty handy with the little one on the way," Eros added.

The chance of a lifetime had presented itself to her. "Of course, I'll take it. Thank you so much, Eros and Marcos." She got up and first shook their hands and then hugged them both. Bewildered beyond belief, she walked back to her chair and kissed Tonio on the cheek.

"That's not all. Tonio, we would like to offer you a job as well. We know that you are a writer and travel agent. We would like to hire you part-time to assist Sidney with slogans and add ideas. I think with the two of you on board, it might be just the lethal dose for our new line coming out soon." Eros sat back, a smile spreading over his face.

Now it was Tonio's turn to be surprised. He had no idea he'd be offered anything. He was happy where he was. "Well, I'm flattered at the proposition. I just don't know."

"We will be happy to wait a few days for your answer. Think it over." Marcos and Eros exchanged glances. "If you did decide to accept the offer, it includes accommodation. Please look out your left window and to the top of the hill. That would be your home."

Sidney looked out the window, and her breath was stolen away from her. It was a little ways away, but from where she sat, she could see it was what dreams were made of. She could imagine her and Tonio sharing a drink before bed and taking in the first-class view of a sunset. It looked to be a one-story rancher with cream-colored stoned walls, wood shutters, and many patios outside. It even looked like it had a waterfall flowing into a possible pool.

What an amazing day, Sidney thought to herself as she squeezed Tonio's leg under the table.

"On second thought . . . I agree to your offer. I know that I can still do my writing job via the Internet. That should give us enough money to get by. What do you think, Sidney?" Tonio asked as he draped his arm around her.

Sidney gave a little squeal of delight and threw her arms around Tonio. She loved him so much. All her dreams were coming true. "It sounds wonderful."

Epilogue

Sidney felt the contractions start at around 1:15 a.m. She hadn't been able to sleep at all. She knew in her subconscious that something was about to happen. The pains were sharp and were coming closer together as the hours went by. At 3:00 a.m., she awoke Tonio who was oblivious to her condition.

Sidney nudged him with her elbow. "Tonio! Wake up! It's time."

"Time for what?" Tonio asked sleepily as he reached to turn on the bedside lamp.

"The baby!" Sidney was agitated. "Wake up!"

Tonio suddenly bolted up into a sitting position and stared at her, fear written all over his face. "Now? . . . ," he asked stupidly.

"Yes, now. And don't ask me any more questions. The baby's coming, and we need to get to the hospital. I don't think it'll be long now. Grab the cell phone and call Aunt Thelma and Maurice on our way. Lets get moving."

Tonio quickly grabbed the prepacked bags, made sure that Sidney was moderately OK, and then loaded them into the car. They had an hour drive to the nearest hospital. He went back in for Sidney and helped her outside and into the vehicle. She was almost screaming with the pain now.

"Just hang in there, sweetie, it won't be long till we're at the hospital," Tonio said as much for his benefit as well for her.

Sidney grabbed the "oh shit" handle on the car and held on tight as another contraction ripped through her stomach. *They don't tell you how bad this feels*, she thought to herself.

They'd been on the road for half an hour. Tonio was trying to drive as fast as he could around the hairpin turns without endangering them.

"Tonio, I'm not going to make it. You have to pull over right now."

Tonio looked at her quickly. "But I'm not a doctor, Sidney."

"Now!" Sidney yelled.

Tonio pulled the car off into the nearest rest area. It was so dark, only the full moon and stars expressed any light.

He ran to the back of the trunk and pulled out the blankets he and Sidney carried in case of emergency picnics, as well as a flashlight. Placing them on the ground, he went and collected Sidney. She could barely walk and almost collapsed on the blankets. She screamed as another contraction seized her. When she could catch her breath, she hissed at Tonio to call the hospital.

With her contractions almost one on top of the other, she felt the urge to push, so she did.

"Yes, Doctor, she's going to have the baby right here on the side of the road. I have no idea what I'm doing. Yes. Yes. Sidney, did your water break?"

"Obviously!" was all she could get out.

Tonio ran and brought back one of the suitcases and rummaged through it until he found anything that could be used as extra towels.

Tonio took off her underwear and shined the flashlight as the doctor instructed.

"Oh god! Yes, Doctor. I see the baby's head. OK." Tonio then spoke to Sidney. "He say's push as hard as you can with every contraction. You can do it, sweetie."

Sidney screamed as the next contraction hit. She pushed with all her might, then again and again and again. It was all that was needed. Tonio caught the little one in one of his shirts and then used a nightgown to clean up the baby and clear the air passages. The baby let out a little cry, and both Sidney and Tonio smiled tears of joy.

"What is it?" Sidney anxiously asked.

Tonio shined the flashlight down, surprised with himself that he hadn't thought to look before. "It's a girl."

Tonio brought their little girl up to meet her mom. He gently placed her on her chest. Just then, they heard the sirens; the ambulance had finally arrived.

At the hospital, cozy in their room, Aunt Thelma and Maurice, now Grandma and Grandpa, met the baby.

"What's her name?" they asked together.

"Adriana Bianca Papadopoulos," Tonio said, smiling. "I know ... it's a mouthful."

"She's so beautiful." Aunt Thelma cooed as she held Adriana close to her.

"Who would have thought all this would have happened two years ago." Maurice leaned down and kissed the bright-eyed baby on the forehead.

"I'm happier than I've ever been in my whole life," Sidney said, starting to cry. Tonio leaned down and kissed his wife on the forehead.

"I know the feeling. I can't wait to see what's going to happen next!"

Aunt Thelma laid the baby down into her mom's awaiting arms. They all sat back and watched mother and daughter fall asleep together.

I hope you enjoyed my story! Stay tuned for my next novel. K. C. Hawkins

Get Published, Inc!
Thorofare, NJ 08086
21 August 2009
BA2009233